MW01120224

the girlfriend's secret

Thirsty Thursday Book 3

kyle autumn

the girlfriend's secret
Copyright © 2018 Kyle Autumn
All rights reserved.
First Edition

No part of this book may be reproduced or transmitted in any form or means, electronic or mechanical, including photocopying, recording, or by any information storage and retrieval systems, without written permission from the author, except for the use of brief quotations in a review.

This is a work of fiction. Names, characters, places, and incidents either are the product of the author's imagination or are used fictitiously, and any resemblance to actual persons, living or dead, business establishments, events, or locales is entirely coincidental.

ISBN: 9781719994767

OTHER BOOKS BY KYLE AUTUMN

DEDICATION

This is dedicated to
all the girls who fall in love
with each other.

CHAPTER 1

Zo

Like the coward I am, I run out of Lyra's hospital room. Once I'm out of sight, I lean against the wall, bring a hand to my forehead, and sigh out a deep breath. I wasn't ready. We've talked about it and talked about it—then talked about it some more. But I just couldn't say the words. Not when I didn't know how everyone would react. They were stuck in my throat, and then the doctor interrupted the moment, so I took it as a sign. And I left. Ugh.

Patti comes out of the room, hot on my heels. "What happened in there?" she asks, her hands out to her sides. "I thought we were finally going to tell them today."

"We were," I admit, kicking off the wall. Then I start walking toward the elevator. "But it didn't seem like the right time. So I choked up."

"I noticed." When we get on the elevator, she faces me and stares me right in the eyes. Once the doors have closed, she asks, "Do you not want to tell them? Because, if you don't, I—"

"Yes!" I rush out. "Yes, I do. I really do. I swear."

"Then what the hell is going on?" she asks, crossing her arms over her chest. "We can't keep this from them forever. It's been long enough already."

When I don't say anything for a moment, she raises an

eyebrow at me.

"I know," I tell her on a deep exhale. "I know, okay? I don't know what you want me to say."

The elevator doors open, but Patti doesn't make a move to leave. I can only take her disappointed glare for so long though. So, before the doors close, I step out onto the first floor and head toward the exit whether she's following me or not. I have to get out of here.

I get it. I fucked up. I dropped the ball. This was supposed to be the day we came clean. And, honestly, I'm tired of living a lie. Keeping a secret. In theory, I'm more than ready to tell everyone. Lyra, Shiree, Chaz, Blake… Even my parents, though it scares the absolute shit out of me. And I'm beyond sorry that my chickenshit attitude has made Patti keep this from them too. She deserves so much better than to keep my secrets.

But, without knowing how they'll react, I'm not sure I can say anything yet. I can't handle the unknown when it comes to something this big. It could be life-altering, mind-blowing, and earth-shattering news. And we'd have to start at the beginning. I'm just not sure I want everyone in my business, and telling people is a guaranteed way to make them look at me differently. I hate to say it, but I'm still not ready for that. Which is why I'm ready to tell everyone but still unwilling to go through with it.

Once we reach my car, I go to get into the driver's seat. But, instead of going to the passenger's side door to go home, Patti follows me. Carpooling was a great idea on the way here, but now, I'm regretting the decision. It's only going to make me face this. Whether I'm ready or not.

"Hey," she says, her hand on my arm to stop me. "We need to talk about this. Because I can't keep doing this with you, Zo."

The use of my actual name hits me right in the gut. I almost can't remember the last time she called me that. It's been Zed ever since high school. So it almost sounded like an insult to my ears. She's serious, and she means business. Shit.

I face her and take a deep, steadying breath. "I know we do." My hands are shaking, and I just want to crawl inside a hole and hide. "I hate that you've had to keep this secret with me, but I don't want anyone judging me or..."

She lets my arm go by sliding it down to my hand and clasping my fingers. "Or what? You have to tell me so I can help you get through this."

Closing my eyes, I squeeze her hand. When I open them, I say, "Or...not loving me anymore."

Her shoulders slump forward as she exhales a whoosh of breath. "Oh, Zed. That's never going to happen," she says, pulling me into a tight hug. When she pulls back, she holds my cheeks in her hands. "You're still you no matter what, okay? Everyone will still love you. Including me. I promise."

I nod as a tear slips down my cheek.

"And, if for some unlikely, ridiculous-ass reason they don't," she continues, making me smile a little, "then you don't need them in your life anyway. But I don't think you'll run into that problem."

Again, I nod, and another tear falls down my other cheek.

She wipes them away for me using her thumbs. "And who cares? You'll always have me." Her lips curve up into a grin. "I've even proven to be more than you can handle sometimes. What more could you possibly ask for?"

At that, I break into a small laugh. Because it's true. She's my best friend, and I don't know what I'd do without her. But, if I don't grow a pair soon and give my secret up, I'll find out exactly what I'd do without her. Which is a much scarier thought than anyone's judgment or lack of love. I'd be so lost and alone. If I don't have to be, I don't want to be. So I decide to grow those balls.

Right now, apparently. Because it's now or never. We

agreed on today, so today it will be.

"I couldn't ask for anything more, Patti." With tear-stained cheeks, I shake my head a little. "Nothing at all."

Then, with Shiree and Chaz approaching their car, which is parked right next to mine, I lean forward and kiss my girlfriend on her soft, sweet lips. For everyone to see for the first time.

***

Patti

Well, this was unexpected. The woman I love more than life itself has her lips on mine in broad daylight. I'm so conditioned not to do this that I freeze for a second. But then I unfreeze and take hold of the moment by sliding my hands into her hair and deepening the kiss. I've waited for this moment for over nine months—for most of my life, really. Of course I'm going to take advantage, sear it into my brain for all of eternity, and make the absolute most of it.

I run my tongue across the seam of her lips, and she lets me in. She always does. It's my favorite way to kiss her, but I'm finding that it's even sweeter with the sun on my skin. Or maybe it's the footsteps I hear approaching us that make this better. Someone else in the world, even if it's a stranger, knows we're together. It's not even a voyeurism thing, and I don't particularly want them to watch us. But someone knows. Someone besides us. Thank the lord.

Her palms grip my back, and her short nails dig into my shoulder blades. But it's almost too hard. To the point of pain. I pause our kiss, about to pull away from her, when I open my eyes. Hers are wide open too, but they're not aimed at me. They're aimed over my shoulder. So maybe she doesn't want strangers watching us kiss yet. That's okay with me. Someone has, and right now, that's enough. But I'm curious who had the pleasure, so I unstick our faces and

4

twist around.

Only to find two people who are decidedly not strangers staring at us.

"Wh...wh...what?" Shiree squeals, throwing her arms out to her sides. "What is going on?" Turning to Chaz, she asks, "Babe, what is going on?"

"Well, Shiree, it looks like Patti and Zo were—"

"I know what it looks like!" she exclaims, interrupting her husband. "I have two eyes. I saw what happened. What I don't understand is why it's happening."

Zo is frozen, stock-still, so I grab her hand to encourage her. When she looks at me, all of her fear pours out of her gaze. All I want to do is wrap her up and keep her safe. Make sure nothing bad happens to her. Ever. But I can't. And these are our friends. Even though Shiree's reaction was, well, unexpected, I don't think it's going to be bad. So I squeeze her fingers and raise my eyebrows a couple of times.

"It's okay, Zed. I'm right here," I remind her, giving her a small smile. "You can do this."

She takes a deep breath, which comes out on a shudder. "Well..." Then she stops.

While I squeeze her hand again, Shiree looks at Chaz with wide eyes. He just shrugs and faces us again, so she does too.

"Spit it out, Zo," she says, taking her husband's hand. "Is it cancer? A brain tumor? Just tell us already!" Tears pool in her eyes, and she wipes at them.

Zo's jaw falls open, and her eyebrows draw down on her forehead. But nothing comes out of her mouth. So I speak up for her.

"What the hell?" I shove my hands on my hips. "Why do you think she is sick? Because she wouldn't be with me if she wasn't dying?"

"B-be with you?" Shiree stutters out. "Like...you two..." She waves a finger between the two of us.

5

"You're...together?"

"That's what it looked like to me," Chaz says, putting his arm around his wife. "I hear that's what two people do when they're together."

"I know that," she grinds out between clenched teeth, swinging her gaze to Chaz. "But I want to know why they couldn't just tell us that."

"We're right here," I remind her, my heart pounding from the anger coursing through my veins. I wanted us to finally tell everyone, but if we're going to get shit from the people we love, we could have kept it to ourselves. "We can hear you."

She faces us again and clears her throat, blinking slowly. Then she approaches Zo and takes her free hand, the one I'm not holding. "Zo. Sweetie. Tell me two things."

Zo, in her state of frozen shock, nods. I grip her hand tighter for some strength. It's not that I think whatever Shiree is about to ask will be bad. I just know my girl. And, right now, she needs it.

"You and Patti are dating?" Shiree asks, staring my girl right in her eyes.

Again, after a short bit of hesitation, Zo nods at her.

"And you don't have cancer?"

This time, she shakes her head.

"Or a brain tumor?"

More head shaking.

"Or any other life-threatening disease?"

One more head shake.

"Oh thank god!" Shiree shouts before throwing herself at Zo and wrapping her arms around her.

I stumble back from the exertion and lose her hand, but she seems fine after a moment of more shock. She even returns Shiree's hug. And I can't help but smile at seeing two of my favorite people in the world so happy. I think I might even see happy tears falling from Shiree's eyes. I definitely see some in Zo's, but they're likely also tears of relief. Mine? They're tears of pride.

"When you left like that, we were too caught up with Lyra and the baby to think about it," Shiree says, pulling back from Zo to look at her. "But then, when Chaz and I were walking to the car, I went back to it, thought about it, and thought the worst! We couldn't think of why you couldn't possibly tell us what was going on with you." Then she goes back in for another hug, this time flailing her other arm at me so I'll join them.

Gladly, I wrap my arms around my girl and our friend. Shiree squeezes us so tight that I can barely breathe, but we're all laughing at the sheer ridiculousness that is this misunderstanding. And it's about relief. Shiree's relieved that Zo's not dying. Zo's relieved that the secret is out and her friends still love her. Well, some of them, but one set down, another to go. And I'm relieved that Zo's worst-case scenario didn't come true. I knew that it wouldn't, but some people have to go through it in order to believe it. I wasn't scared, which is why I pushed. But fear is a tricky bitch for Zo. I'm just glad to be the one by her side to help her through it.

Chaz decides to join the hug by embracing all three of us at once. "I'm glad you're okay, Zo." He squeezes us tighter and then ruins everything. "I had no idea you two were lesbians though."

"Oh my god!" all three of us say to him at the same time, and we all break the hug up.

"It's not even like that," Zo clarifies. "We're just two people who happened to"—she slides her gaze to me—"fall in love."

Right here in the parking lot of the hospital, my heart swells. It's full of pride, love, and joy. All thanks to this woman standing next to me. She's the best thing that's ever happened to me, and I have no idea what I'd do without her.

"I love you too, Zed." I bring her hand to my lips and

kiss it.

Her shy grin sets my soul on fire. Always has, always will.

"Well, now that that's out of the way," Shiree says, "come back to the house with us! I have to get back to my babies, but I want to hear all about how this"—she waves that finger between us again—"happened."

Zo looks at me, one eyebrow up in a curious expression. I shrug with one shoulder, telling her that it's her call. Maybe it's best if we have a trial run at this. Get one instance of telling someone our story under our belt before the heavy-hitters, like her parents, come into play.

Once she agrees, Shiree claps her hands. "Yay! We'll see you there!" She turns toward her car. But then, halfway around, she freezes, looking like an idea—a bad one—has struck her. "Wait!" she exclaims, slowly pivoting back to face us and holding a finger up in the air. "Tell me just one more thing."

"Okay," Zo and I both hesitantly say.

Shiree puts a hand on her hip. "Does Lyra already know? You two didn't tell her first, right?"

CHAPTER 2

Patti

When Zo and I arrive at Shiree and Chaz's house, we're still laughing about how she was worried she was the last to know something big. We reminded her that she knew about Lyra's baby before we did, but she reminded us that Lyra told us about Blake first. Honestly, I don't care who knew what when. I'm glad Zo's laughing though. She was afraid that all of that was going to go so much differently, but it didn't. Shiree's concern lay with Zo's health, not her questionable sexual orientation.

Inside the house, baby cries fill the space. Zo's immediate reaction is to go straight for the babies. Which works for the leaving babysitter, who passes the one she has off to Shiree before she heads out the door. But the other baby in a carrier shrieks until Zo lifts him out and holds him in her arms. As she rocks him, she coos and rubs his back, and he calms and quiets down.

"Wow," Shiree breathes out while holding her daughter. "Harlan's never calmed down that quickly for me. I don't know if I should be impressed and relieved that it happened that fast or pissed that he doesn't do that for me."

"Zo must be the baby whisperer," Chaz says, leaning in to check on his daughter. "At least you're not that fussy, right, Lara?" He smiles at his wife. "We got one good kid.

She won't give us any trouble."

"Until she's fifteen and wants to date," I mutter under my breath, grinning.

"Oh lord. Don't remind him," Shiree groans. "We have way too much time before he needs to worry about that." Then she hands Lara over to Chaz, who looks like he's about to explode.

With a red face, he grits out, "She's not dating until she's thirty-five. And that's if she's lucky."

Shiree laughs and pats his back. "Okay, honey." She pecks him on the cheek.

He just shakes his head and walks away with his daughter. "Thirty-five," he grumbles. "You hear me, little girl?"

Zo giggles lightly, still rocking a now-sleeping Harlan. She brings him up to her shoulder and cups his little head. "Should we put him down?" she asks Shiree.

She nods and holds her hands out. "I'll be right back," she whispers as she carefully takes her son out of Zo's arms.

Zo smiles to her, but something's missing. I think it's the usual light in her eyes. So I give her a gentle poke in the ribs.

"Hey. You okay?" I ask her.

Distractedly, she says, "Hmm?" while staring at Shiree as she walks away with the baby. Then she shakes her head. "Oh, yeah. I'm fine."

"I know that look. You're not fine," I say, tucking some of her red hair behind her ear.

She tries to wave a dismissive hand, but my other hand comes up to her face.

I cup her cheeks to get her to look at me. "Whatever it is, you can tell me. You know that."

A tear shines in her right eye. For whatever reason, it's the one that always tears up first. And that's her tell. When that happens, I know that something's wrong. But she's a tightly locked secret-keeper. It takes a lot to get stuff out of her. So it's a wonder I ever got her to admit her feelings for me.

But I did. And here we are, at our friends' house, about to explain the whole thing. I'm so proud of my girl that butterflies threaten to take my stomach over. Instead, it lurches at the thought of something being wrong with her.

"I do know that. Later, okay?" she asks, pleading with me with her gaze.

After I give her a long stare, I nod. "Okay." Then I kiss her lips. Because I'm able to do that in front of whoever I want now. And the butterflies do end up taking over.

"Oh boy. It's gonna take a while to get used to that," Shiree says as she enters the front room again.

Zo breaks away from me and covers her mouth with her hand. I get it though, so I won't let it bother me. She's not used to it yet. Frankly, neither am I, but that's the thing about love. It doesn't matter if it's wrong or right for anyone else.

"But you'll get used to it," I tell her, taking Zo's hand.

Shiree nods. Then she claps—quietly so she doesn't wake the baby—and gestures to the different places to sit around the room. "Get comfy, because I wanna hear all about it!"

As Zo and I sit on the couch together, I say, "Lyra's gonna be upset."

"Psh," Shiree replies, taking a seat on the chair across from us. "She just had her baby. She needs time to rest." Then she makes a shoo motion with her hands. "Go on. Tell me everything while Chaz watches the babies."

I look at Zo. She's been terrified of this for months. We've had a close call or two, but it's all coming to a head now. And I know she's strong enough for it, but her worries make it hard for her to say the words. Now that we're here, I don't mind doing the talking. She did her part and took that leap. Kissed me in front of the world. I can take the wheel now.

"Okay," I say, taking Zo's hand and placing our interlaced fingers on my lap. Then I turn my attention to Shiree. "We'll start at the beginning."

***

Zo

Nine months ago

Thirsty Thursday. My favorite night of the week. I love getting together with my girlfriends. And it's been a great night—even if all we've done is laugh at Shiree's expense. The whole situation with Charles Masters, local billionaire, is rather humorous. Even Shiree thinks so. But it's obvious that something more is going on, whether she wants to believe it or not. She's never been this caught up in, well, anything before. She's had her fair share of things to get caught up in, too. But it's never been like this.

"I'm not sure strange begins to cover it," Patti says, pointing at Shiree with her beer bottle. "But what are you gonna do now?"

"Umm…" Shiree says, drawing the word out. "Order another round?"

I was hoping she'd actually answer the question, but maybe she's not ready to face this stuff yet. Oh well. She's off doing exactly what she said she was going to do before I can press her for more info. Then Lyra runs after her and it's just Patti and me.

Which, if I'm honest, is the way I prefer it. It's always kind of been Shiree and Lyra and then Patti and me. The other two work together, so they see each other more often. It's given them more opportunity to be closer to each other than they are with us. Which is fine. Patti and I go way back, so we're used to it being the two of us.

Except, this time, when Lyra and Shiree are gone, Patti gives me a weird look. One I've seen her make before, but never has it been directed at me. Or any other woman she's met, as far as I know.

I tug my pursed lips to the side. "What?" I ask her.

She swigs a sip from her beer—her third, which doesn't include the shots she's taken—and sets the bottle on the table, tipping it slightly in my direction. "You."

Raising an eyebrow, I point to myself. "Me? What about me?"

"You just care a lot. I like that." She shrugs. Her dark, wavy bob sways with the motion.

"Okay," I reply slowly, circling my hands around my glass. But I'm smiling.

I do care. Probably too much. It's nice that she noticed though. And it feels good that she likes it too. It's generally a frowned-upon quality. Caring too much means being in too deep. Giving too much of myself too soon. I think that's something Shiree, Lyra, and I have in common. Patti? Not so much. So it's nice that she's acknowledged it and appreciates it.

We've been friends for so long, so I'm not sure why she's bringing it up now, but maybe it's the beer talking. It's nothing new. I've always worried and cared more than I should. And I should have learned my lesson by now, that it doesn't get me anywhere, because I'm single and doomed to be a crazy cat lady.

Ugh. Here I go again. Worrying about the future. Caring more than I should. What does Patti always tell me?

"Come back to now, Zed." She snaps her fingers in front of my face.

My eyes go wide. "Whoa. I was literally just trying to remember that phrase." Then my lips curve up into a grin. "You know, you're always saying and doing the right thing for me. And I like that about you."

Maybe the alcohol tonight is talking for both of us. Or maybe I've realized I need to appreciate Patti more than I do.

As she scrunches her nose, she gives me a small, crooked smile. "You do?"

I tilt my head at her. "Is my best friend being shy?"

Her smile falls before she takes a large chug of her beer, which drains the bottle. "Me? Never," she deadpans.

That's exactly what I thought. But the way she said it has me concerned. Because that's what I do. Worry. So I'll leave it alone. I'm probably being too sensitive, and no one likes Negative Nancy.

I don't have time to worry about whether or not I should worry though. Shiree and Lyra are back, and they set the drinks on the table, clearly in the middle of a conversation.

"Discredit what?" I ask to discover what that conversation was about.

"Yeah." Patti points her empty bottle at me. "What Zo said."

Oh no. She said Zo and not Zed. Something really is wrong. I was right to worry. And I try to give her a look, but Lyra gives us the scoop and then Shiree wants to dance. So we all grab our drinks and head to the dance floor.

Once we get there, Patti downs her fourth beer. She sets it on the nearest table then throws her hands in the air, dancing circles around Lyra and Shiree. When she makes her way back to me, I tap her on her shoulder.

"Hey!" I yell over the music while doing something that barely counts as dancing. "What's going on with you?"

"Nothing!" she shouts back, twisting and dancing. "Nothing is going on with me. Why would you think that?"

I shrug one shoulder. "Well, you called me Zo, for one."

"That's who you are, isn't it? You're Zo," she spits out, slurring her words a little, before spinning around in a circle. "You'll always be Zo."

I stop pretending to dance. "I don't even know what that means, Patti." Then I try to sway my hips again. "Of course I'm Zo. But, to you, I'm Zed."

She throws her arms out to her sides. "And that's what's wrong with the world!"

Again, I freeze. "You're drunk and not making any sense."

"Oh, no," she says, shaking her head. "I'm making perfect sense. It's not my fault you don't understand." Then she wags a finger at me.

That's it. I've had enough of whatever the hell she's doing. We're going to leave and get to the bottom of it because I'm way too worried about her now. I don't think I've ever seen her act this way, and we've known each other for half of our lives. That's fourteen years of being Zed, only Zo when she's mad at me. And I haven't done anything wrong tonight. Have I? Shit. I don't think I have. Either way, I've had enough of this.

Once I reach Shiree and Lyra, I get close to Lyra's ear and shout over the music. "Patti's not feeling so hot! So I'm gonna take her home!"

Shiree looks at me, asking what I said to Lyra with her eyes. I put my hands on my stomach, hook my thumb in Patti's direction, and frown. When they both pout, I wave them off and turn my frown into a small smile. Then we all say goodbye before they go back to dancing and I drag Patti off the dance floor and out the door.

"What the hell?" she squeals when we're on the sidewalk.

I spin around and face her, pointing at her with my index finger. "You're gonna tell me what's going on with you right now."

She puts her hands on her hips and pops one hip out to the side. "Oh wow. It's assertive Zed now, huh?"

"Well, I've had enough, so here she is," I spit back.

"Good," she slurs. "I like that about you too."

"Great, Patti. Just tell me what you're doing." I cross my arms over my chest. "Why are you so drunk tonight?"

"Because I can't take it anymore!" she yells, her arms

thrown out to her sides.

"Can't take what?" I push, mirroring what she's doing with her arms. "I don't understand what you're being so cryptic about!"

Her arms fall against her body, and she lets out a deep breath, her shoulders slumping forward. She looks completely defeated, and the bar's neon lights highlight the sheen of sweat on her forehead. And then I have another one of those strange urges I've been trying to ignore for a while. The kind where I want to push her hair out of her face, cup her cheek, and comfort her in a way that would cross our friendship line. But, before I can even acknowledge it, let alone shake it off, she speaks up.

After another long breath in, she looks straight at me and hits me right in the heart with her words. On a rush of air, she says, "This really isn't how I wanted to tell you I'm in love with you."

CHAPTER 3

Patti

I'd kiss her right now if it weren't the absolute worst thing I could do after having said that. I may be drunk, and drunk words may be sober thoughts, but I have enough wits about me not to totally fuck this up.

Well, maybe I did fuck it up. I don't know yet. She's just standing there, staring at me like I have three heads. Her mouth opens like she's about to speak, but she doesn't say anything yet.

God, it felt so damn good to get out though. I've held that in for way longer than I should have. And it's out there now. Nothing I can do it about. Can't take it back. It may completely change our relationship in the worst way and I may completely lose her, but twelve years is far too long to keep something like that to myself.

Just when I think she's going to respond, she closes her mouth back up. Then she lets her arms fall to her sides, spins around, and rushes off toward her car. We drove together, so it's not like she's going anywhere without me. But she's obviously trying to run away from this, and I'm just drunk enough to not let her.

"Hey," I say, grabbing for her arm. "Shouldn't we talk about that?" I jut a thumb in the direction of the bar.

She wrenches herself out of my grasp. "Get in the car,

Patti."

I start to respond, but she holds a hand up and closes her eyes.

"No. Don't. Just get in the car."

When she opens them again, she finds the driver's side door handle and yanks the door open. Then she throws herself behind the steering wheel. As she starts the car, I get in next to her. The car begins to spin, so I shut my eyes. But that doesn't help. My stomach turns, so I blink my eyes open, and then the whole world spins.

Zo backs the car out of our parking spot and takes off. The world stops spinning, but the speed at which she's driving upsets my stomach more. With no other options, I suck in a deep breath and close my eyes again, gripping the armrest and the center console to keep myself as steady as I can. Then everything quiets and disappears, and I swear I feel the weight of her hand on mine as I slip off to sleep.

~~~

Why the hell does my mouth taste so bad? More important is why the hell my head hurts so bad. When I bring my hand to my head and realize I'm still wearing last night's clothes and not in my bed, an even more important question comes to mind: Where am I?

Once I've finally pried my sleep-crusty eyes open, I see Zo's purse on Zo's side table by Zo's door. On my right are Zo's loveseat and Zo's lamp. Everything is Zo's. I'm at her place?

Then last night hits me like a Mack truck. Holy shit. That wasn't a dream; that's a memory. I actually said those words to my best friend. Words I've kept hidden for almost half of my life. Feelings I've pushed down to make sure I have her in my life in some capacity. Because I almost tried pushing that conversation once. And, when I got my answer, I decided not to go there ever again. It wasn't worth losing her over, even though it meant I'd be unhappy for the rest of my life.

From Zo's bed, I watch her sit on the floor and pick a polish for her toes. She does this before every date she goes on, and because she's eighteen and gorgeous, she goes on a lot of them. Well, a lot to me is any at all when you consider the fact that I've never gone on one. Being in love with your best friend kind of makes you not want to go on dates with other people.

"Which color should I pick this time?" she asks me. It's an innocent question coming from her, but she doesn't realize what it does to me.

I've gotten good at pretending though. The last year and a half has given me a lot of practice opportunities.

"Ummm," I say, stretching the word out while I count to five in my brain. "Well, what's he like?" It's torture, but it's the kind of thing a best friend would do.

"He's so cute," she breathily replies, hiding behind her hands. Then her hands drop and she stares off into space. "But I'm not sure he's all that smart."

Secretly, I'm grinning because I don't think this guy has a snowball's chance in Hell. But, if she asks, I'm grinning because it's ridiculous that she's giving this guy a shot at all. Obviously, he's not good enough for her. And a best friend would say that. Just not the same way a jealous potential lover would.

I flip a page of my magazine. "Then go for purple."

"Why?" She puts the green down though and unscrews the purple bottle's cap.

What I want to say is that purple looks best on her. That's why I suggested it before thinking it through. I can't think of a reason why she should pick purple over green because she doesn't think the guy's smart. The hell am I supposed to say?

Somehow, I settle for, "Because, if he's smart, he'll notice purple."

She thinks about it for a moment and then starts to paint her nails. "Because what guy doesn't notice green? It's the color of money." Then she nods and looks at me. "You're so smart."

Her smile slays me. She has no idea how gorgeous she is, and I want to tell her every day. I want her to know how important and special she is. So I decide to hedge a little.

"Smart because I know my worth. I don't know why you put up with guys like that, Zed."

She shrugs and paints her third toe. "It's just one date. Who knows what could happen. Maybe I'm wrong."

"You're almost never wrong," I say, shaking my head. "You worry too much to guess at things, and you don't do things you aren't sure about."

Again, she shrugs. "I guess."

"Well, maybe you should do something you're not sure about," I offer. Then I peek over the top of my magazine. "Like go on a date with a girl next time."

She freezes. The polish brush hovers over her toe, and she stays that way until a glob of paint splatters onto her nail. That snaps her out of her trance, so she quickly puts the brush back in the bottle and reaches for a cotton ball to wipe the paint off. As she does, she shakes her head.

"No. That'll never happen," she states simply. Then, with emphasis, "Ever."

But there's something else there. Because her right eye tears up and she swipes at it before the tear falls. Behind my magazine, though, I didn't miss that. I don't know what it means, but her words shut me up. I go back to flipping pages and allowing my heart to break even more while she paints her toenails for a date with someone else.

Perched on the edge of her couch, with my head in my hands, I shake myself from the memory. When I open my eyes, those very toes come into view—thankfully free of polish. I raise my gaze and find a cup of coffee in her hands and a nervous look on her face.

"You okay?" she asks, dressed in her usual work scrubs. "I've been—"

"Worried about me?" I finish for her, reaching for the cup.

She nods.

I do too. But then I wince. The movement felt like my brain was smashing against my skull.

Zo sits next to me and puts her hand on my back. Her

warmth seeps through my shirt and comforts me in a way the coffee can't. It also hurts in a way coffee can't hurt me though.

"Why don't you just lie back down?" she asks.

After a sip of my coffee—sugar and a dash of cocoa, exactly how I like it—I very gently shake my head while gazing at the floor. "I'll be fine."

When she takes her hand back, the loss of her heat chills me to the bone. Then she sets both hands in her lap and interlaces her fingers, staring a hole in the carpet.

"Hey," I say slowly. Awkwardly. "About what I said last night…"

She sucks in a big breath and shakes her head. "You were drunk. It's okay. Let's just forget it."

My shoulders slump forward. Sure, I thought I could explain, maybe shed some light on it. Perhaps even get some closure so I could shut the whole thing down somehow. Yeah, I've tried for years and every attempt has been unsuccessful. But I finally admitted it and she's choosing to ignore it. I'm not sure yet if that hurts worse than being shot down. That would at least have been a solid answer compared to this never knowing the truth. Unless she's sparing my feelings. But this isn't sparing anything. Now, I'm more torn up than I was last night, and that's saying something.

Would a best friend let this slide? Or would she pursue the conversation anyway? Honestly, I don't know. All I know is I don't want to lose her. So I shut my mouth. The truth is out there. I guess it's up to her to decide what to do with it.

***

Zo

Bringing her back to my place was a no-brainer. What's

not is what to do about what she said last night. She was drunk. That's not even a question. But I've known her too long not to believe her. Love can mean many things, and there are different kinds of love. Yet she didn't say that she loves me. She said that she's in love with me. And that's very, very different.

I could be cautious and say that I heard her wrong. Maybe something got lost in translation and I misheard what she'd said. But I saw it in her eyes too. The words fell off her lips and landed right in my heart. Right in that spot I've always had reserved for her.

Maybe I'm a coward—well, yeah. I'm totally a coward. That's all there is to it. I've built my life to be what was expected of me. Working a steady job, living on my own, and dating men in the hopes of marrying one and having children with him someday. That's how my life is supposed to be.

The problem is that's not what I want. While I enjoy my apartment and my job as a dental assistant, I've tolerated dating. Not because I don't enjoy men. I do, and some of the men I've dated have been great. In and out of bed—because don't get me wrong: I'm no virgin. They just haven't been great for me. No one's great for me.

Except my best friend. But, according to my parents and their beliefs, that would be an abomination. And it'd be an even bigger abomination if their daughter turned out to be a lesbian.

I live and breathe for my parents, seeing as it's a miracle I'm even here. But that's meant living up to their expectations no matter the cost to me. No matter if it means denying myself the one thing I want more than life itself.

It doesn't help that it's a recent development. One I've been trying to dismiss as normal feelings for a best friend. Someone you deeply care about because you've known them so long that they've become a part of you. But, when those feelings and thoughts turned into the romantic kind, I knew I had a problem.

Now, the problem's even bigger. Because I apparently have a shot at making these feelings and thoughts a reality. There's a chance they could come true. But their coming true means possibly losing my family. I have no idea what I'd do without my family. Yet Patti's my family too. I'd been worried about losing her before she admitted how she felt. Now that I know that my feelings are reciprocated, that worry is gone. One less concern is good. The worry of losing my family will never go away.

I've disappointed her though. Her hunched position clearly telegraphs that. By choosing to ignore this, I've put us back in separate boxes. Put us right back to square one. And that's not where she wanted to be, even if I don't know why yesterday was that much different than any other day.

"Look," I tell her as she sips her coffee. "I have to get to work. But feel free to stay as long as you want. Shower…whatever." I rise from the couch and approach the front door.

She brings her legs up onto the couch and bends them to her left, watching me as I get my socks and my shoes on. Her gaze is hot, like a laser beam on me. But I have to ignore it. Coming face-to-face with this won't do me any good right now. So, as I grab my purse, I keep my back turned to her. She stops me with one word though. My favorite word to leave her lips.

"Zed."

The soft syllable roots me to the floor. Pauses my hand above the door handle. Still, I keep my back to her, but I peek over my shoulder. The pain on her face slices into my heart.

"I meant it. You should know."

That's all she says. It's all the clarification she needs to give. No need to specify; we both know what she's referring to. Doesn't matter though. I can't bring myself to acknowledge it. And I'll break if I see how much ignoring her hurts. Instead, I'll spend the rest of the day worrying about how my best friend is feeling, even though I know I have all the power to make her pain go away.

~ ~ ~

At work, I can't get my head in the game. All day, I've called our regulars by the wrong names and spaced out while patients have been talking to me. Even Dr. Phelps had to ask if I was okay, and he usually tries to stay out of his dental assistants' business. I guess I'm just a hot mess today. But I really need my head clear in twenty minutes because that's when I'll be at my parents' house for regular Friday dinner.

The drive over gives me no clarity though. I'm still a hot mess. And I'm an even bigger hot mess when I pull up to their house and discover Patti's car out front. Throughout the years, she's occasionally come to Friday dinner. My family loves her almost as much as they love me, mostly because they didn't want only one child, but that's the hand they were dealt. So, when Patti and I became best friends, they started treating her like she was their own.

And she's been grateful since day one. She was raised by her grandparents when her parents died in a car accident. Then, when her grandparents died, she was on her own. So she's appreciated having my family take her in. It's also been a way for me to keep her close. But it's also why she has to know how seismic what she said to me is. She knows my parents as well as I do, and they won't take too kindly to this. Not in the least.

"Hey, sweetie!" my mom gushes when I walk inside the house. "Dinner's almost ready. I just have to take the rolls out of the oven." As she hugs me, her sweet-smelling perfume envelops me. It's the scent of my childhood, and memories rush into my mind while I embrace her.

Like the times she hugged me before each band concert in high school. The times she brought me soup and tea and felt my forehead when I was sick. And the times she helped me put my backpack on when I was a child. Even the times in my adult life when we've stood next to each other and cooked Friday dinner together. If I admit that I feel for Patti the way she feels for me, will all of those be just what they are—memories?

"Patti's in the kitchen. She told us something pretty interesting, too," she tells me when she pulls away.

My stomach drops to the floor. But I quickly realize that she couldn't have told her about what she said last night. My mother wouldn't be smiling at me if she had. Not knowing where she's going with this has adrenaline rushing through my veins anyway.

She motions for me to follow her into the kitchen. "Why didn't you tell us you are thinking about getting a cat?"

Relief like no other floods through me. Good grief. I told Patti that a couple of weeks ago, but I haven't followed through on it. I'm guessing it was something to talk about so she didn't spill her guts to my mom like she did to me last night. I'm not ready to face her yet though. I could barely look at her this morning, but it's good to know she still feels welcome at my parents' house.

As I trail behind my mom, I say, "I wasn't sure about it yet. I thought I'd tell you when I'd put more thought into it."

"I hope you do," she tells me. "I worry about you being there at your house all alone. Maybe you should get a big dog instead. At least until you get married. Then the man of your dreams will keep you safe."

I roll my eyes at her usual type of comment. Once we reach the kitchen, the smell of stew hits my nose. It's one of my favorite meals she makes, and my stomach starts growling with the anticipation of dipping a roll into the thick soup. After the day I've had, I'm ready to sit back and relax. Enjoy a normal night and a good meal with my parents.

But then my gaze lands on Patti, who's sitting at the table and laughing at something my father must have said. He's stirring the stew for my mom, and his smile toward her melts me a little. I want nothing more than for my father to smile at both me and Patti for the rest of our lives. I'm afraid, though, that my wish won't come true if anything happens between us.

The growls in my stomach turn into knots of fear. However, when Patti turns her attention to me and winks, all seems right with the world. I thought she'd still be in intense-mode, but she's sharing a laugh with my father as my mom sets the table. So I set my purse on the counter and take a seat at the four-person table. Right next to Patti. Where I've always sat.

"Hi, Zoeybell," my dad says when he embraces me. He's called me that since my parents brought me home from the hospital, and even though I'm twenty-eight now, it'll never get old.

"Hey, Dad," I respond, squeezing him tight.

"Patti was just telling me about last night," he informs me when he pulls back.

And there my stomach goes again. Dropping to the floor, tying itself in knots a Boy Scout can't undo.

"She did?" I carefully question, eyeing her.

"Yep. Taking her home after she'd forgotten her limits." With his back to me as he stirs the stew one last time, he says, "You two take such good care of each other. Just like real sisters would." Then he smiles at us. "Who's ready to eat?"

Not me. Not me at all. I'm ready to throw up all over the table. But I won't do that. I'll just keep secrets and worry myself to death instead.

CHAPTER 4

Patti

Dinner went well. She hadn't been expecting me, but that's probably because she didn't check her phone at work. And, even though her parents didn't seem to notice she was acting weird all night, I knew—especially when she barely touched her favorite stew. So, to me, it's no surprise when we leave their house and she tells me we need to talk.

"Follow me to my place, then," I tell her. After what happened last night, I need to sleep in my own bed tonight. And I assume this talk is going to take a while.

The drive there is nerve-racking. Nerves coil in my stomach, but I shut them down. It's just Zo. Zed. My best friend. There's nothing scary about her. Except the fact that she holds my future in the palm of her hand. One word and I'm destroyed. Hopefully, that's in a good way.

When we get to my apartment, I unlock the door for us and let her go in first. She looks around like she hasn't been here before. Like she's not here at least once a week. And I wonder what she's seeing. If my admission has somehow changed her perspective of me, my home, and us. Then I hope that it has changed her. I hope she realizes what she means to me, and I hope that it makes her look at me the same way.

But I know what's at stake here. I know her parents just

as well as she does. They've treated me like their daughter ever since Zo brought me into the fold. And they're the closest thing I have to family. So I really do get it. And I would be putting it on the line too. But she's worth it to me. Worth everything that could come from more than friendship between us.

"Is something different in here?" she asks, hanging her purse on the coatrack by the door. "It looks...neater."

I don't want to admit that I spent part of the day cleaning and dusting in anticipation of her coming by tonight. Sure, she knows I'm kind of a messy person. But she's not, and she needs to see that I'm serious.

"Just cleaned it up a bit in here. It was probably time," I say, laughing a bit. Trying to play it all down.

I don't think I get one past her though. Oh well. There's no point in lying to her now. I bared my soul, so I have nothing else left to hide. Nothing is more important than the truth I told her last night.

Still in her scrubs, she sits in her spot on my futon. It's not lost on me that I have a coatrack but no couch or loveseat like a normal adult. I just like it better. It fits me better. And I've always liked how Zo thought it was cute. So the futon lives on.

"So," she says, her palms on her thighs as she stares a hole into the carpet of my living room.

"Wine?" I ask. It seems like a wine kind of conversation.

"Yes," she rushes out on an exhale, sounding relieved that I asked. Then she freezes, clears her throat, and says, "Please. That'd be great."

"Long day?" That's what I ask instead of any of the other questions shooting through my brain.

She nods as I go into the kitchen to get our drinks. "Something like that."

When I return with two half-full glasses, she accepts one. We clink glasses in an odd "cheers" thing, and then, before I can finish asking her what she wanted to talk about—even though I know full well what she wants to talk about—she downs the entire glass of wine.

"Any chance you have more of that?" she questions, holding her glass out.

I take it from her. "Yes, but"—I set our glasses on the floor next to my feet and then return to my upright position—"not until we have the talk you wanted—"

The next thing I know, her lips are on mine. Her soft, wine-sweet lips. She's kissing me with the lips of my dreams. And I, like a fly to honey, somehow return the kiss instead of stay frozen, rooted to my seat, like part of my brain wants to. No, in an act of mercy, the part of my brain that's wanted this more than anything was allowed to make the decision on how to respond. And respond I do.

I cup her face as we kiss. My heart races and my stomach flutters when she softly moans at my touch. Heat courses through my veins, and a high I've never known nearly brings me to my knees even though I'm already sitting. Though her mouth stays closed, I still love it. It's chaste but sweet. Innocent but perfect. All because it's Zo.

Maybe it's greedy, but I want more. I'll never get enough of her. Yet I can't push her. If it's too fast too soon, I'll lose her every way I have her. So I let her lead while her face is between my hands and her lips take mine.

When she pauses the kiss but leaves her lips against mine, I dare to open my eyes. And what I see takes my breath away. So much so that I break our connect to get a better view. A few inches away, she's utterly serene. A light pink has tinged her cheeks, and she looks relaxed and happy. No worry creases her brow. None. At all. Even after what we just did. I thought she'd be freaking out, but apparently, I don't know my girl—my best friend—like I thought I did.

Not if she just kissed me like it's the only thing in the world she's ever wanted to do. And like it's the only thing in the world she'd fight to keep doing.

"Oh my god," she says, covering her mouth with her hand.

I expected those words. But not the way she said them. I thought they'd come out with shock and fear. Not with the pure reverence she's glowing with. Not with the absolute joy on her face and the love in her eyes.

Maybe I'm reading too much into this. Maybe I'm not though. When I go to ask, however, she puts a finger on my lips to stop me. Then she rises from my futon and holds her hand out. I look up at her, wondering what the hell is going on in her head. But she appears to be a woman on a mission, and I know for certain I'm not going to prevent her mission from being accomplished. Not when I have a feeling I'm the goal of the mission. No way.

When I take her hand, she tugs me up and turns her back to me. She leads me down the hall to my bedroom, and the whole way there, my heart pounds a wild sprint inside my chest. I'm afraid it's going to explode when she pushes my door open and pounces on me again.

This kiss is much more passionate than the one before. She's frantic now. The way I thought I would be when I finally got her in my arms—and this close to my bed. Yet I'm not. I'm straining to keep my head in this. To memorize the way she feels against me. To sear the imprint of her lips on mine. Because I'm not stupid. I'll take this kiss because I'm selfish, but also because I don't expect it to happen ever again.

She presses her front against mine now, so I wrap an arm around her to pull her closer. To test the waters, I open my mouth to see if she'll let me in. Much to my delight, she does. And she tastes like the best things about life. Like all the things I'd die without. I have no idea how I'm going to give this up after this taste.

She slips her hands around my waist, and I run mine up her back and into her hair as I direct us toward my bed. I have no intention of taking this too far, but there's no reason why we can't be more comfortable, right? Only, when I get us there, I start to realize what we're doing.

We're kissing. Zo and I. Kissing. It's not a best-friend move. Even though I love her, adore her with every fiber of my being, I have zero clue where she stands. What state of mind she is in. Yes, I have exactly what I've been dying for for the past twelve years in the palm of my hand, but really, I'm the one in the palm of hers. And she has the ability to crush me with the closing of her fist. Or her mouth. Or herself out of my life.

No. I won't have that. I won't jeopardize having her around by doing something I'm not even sure she's thought through. We were supposed to be talking, not making out. Though this is more than I felt I could ask for, that talk will do so much more for my heart and my mind. That is what I need right now. So, incredibly reluctantly yet fully resolutely, I break away from her mouth and grip her hips.

"Zed, I don't think—" I start to say, but she stops me by shaking her head and kissing me again.

"Just let me have this one night," she requests, pulling me back to her. "One night where my dreams have come true and you're mine."

"I've always been yours," I breathe against her lips without any hesitation. "Always."

It might be a mistake, but it's mine to find out. Considering I've never been good at telling her no, I don't start being good at it now. Instead, I let her find my lips again and pull me down to my bed. Where I kiss her until I forget how much it'll kill me when it's all over.

***

Zo

She feels so right pressed up against me. Her lips are like heaven on mine. Being with her is everything I hoped it would be and more. But I can feel her hesitation. Her reluctance to give herself to me for the night. I just need this one night so I can have a taste of this. So I'll know for sure exactly what I'll be missing out on for the rest of my life.

It's crazy. I know that. Why torture myself by capturing these memories to keep forever? Why tempt myself with one hit and risk becoming an addict? The short answer is that I've never, ever let myself before. And, now, I have to. I have this inexplicable pull toward her. And I can't control it now that I know how she feels about me. I want this one night where I can let go, not worry about a thing, and be me. We can be Patti and Zed the way we were always meant to be for this one night.

And then—no. I'm not thinking about tomorrow. Only about tonight. That's it.

I let her take the lead. I have no clue what to do with a woman, though I won't say I'm any better with a man. Sexual encounters haven't been high on my list when the one person I've wanted them with lately was off-limits. I've heard her stories though. Best friends tell each other that kind of stuff, so I know exactly what she's capable of. And I want it all.

She starts to creep her hand under my scrub top, and her light, small hands are perfect on my bare skin. Her lips trail down my neck as she inches my shirt up until I lift my arms as a sign of permission to take my shirt off. Which we do. Then my hands go to the hem of hers, and I raise that up and over her head. Though I've seen her this way countless times—in a bra—I haven't had the opportunity to freely admire how beautiful she is. Awkwardly stolen glances here and there—that's been it. But, right now, I feast on the sight of her.

Patti seems to do the same in return. Her gaze roams over my bra-covered chest and down my torso. All the way to my waist and my hips, where my scrub bottoms start. The heat of her stare begins to make me self-conscious, but I take a deep inhale and let her look. I want her to see me. All of me. So I hook my thumbs into the waistband of my bottoms, my panties included, and push them down, squirming on the bed as I go.

When she realizes what I'm doing, she helps me. Her hands join mine in their mission, and once my clothes have been tossed aside, I unbutton her jeans. To get them all the way off, she stands up and shimmies them down her legs until she's as bare as I am. I sit up on the bed and scoot to perch on the edge to get a better look at her. Head to toe, she's gorgeous. And I knew she would be. Seeing it in real life though? Having her right in front of me and not just naked in my mind?

"Hey," she softly coos, reaching toward my face. She swipes a tear from my right eye with her thumb. "Come back to now, Zed. Stay with me."

I sniffle a little and nod, leaning in toward her touch. Adrenaline zips through me, and my thoughts race at a million miles an hour, but I shut it all down to be in the now with her. Cupping my cheek, she straddles me, so I scoot backwards to make room for her there. Then she cups my other cheek and kisses my lips. As her fingers slide into my hair, I bring my arms around her.

"I don't know what to do," I admit against her mouth between kisses.

"Whatever feels right," she whispers. "Just do that. Anything you want."

After another deep, cleansing breath, I trail my hands up her sides and over to the clasp of her bra. As I unhook it, she does the same with mine. Straps fall down our shoulders, and we take turns removing the rest of the material. When our breasts are free, we return to each other and they brush from the nearness. Instantly, my nipples harden and a wetness forms between my legs. It's a rather foreign feeling, considering I've never been this turned on with anyone I've ever been with. And I can tell I'm already addicted to the pleasure. All she has to do is look at me and I'm a puddle of desire for her.

With that desire rolling through me, I chance reaching up and caressing her bare breasts. I've only ever touched my own, but hers feel just right in my hands. I sweep my thumbs over her stiff peaks, loving how hard they are for me. Goose bumps break out over her skin, which gives me the courage to bring one of her nipples to my mouth. Going with whatever feels right seems to be working, because she moans and grinds against me, gently tugging my hair to pull me closer.

I suck lightly, swirling my tongue around her nipple as men have done to me. Then I release it and move over to the other one, giving it fair attention. Gripping her hips, I nuzzle between her breasts and breathe her in. This moment is so sweet, so perfect. I don't ever want to lose it. And, suddenly, tears overtake me.

She leans back and holds my face in her palms, watching me carefully. Once she's placed a sweet, calming kiss on my lips, she rises, walks around the bed, and pulls the covers back. When she gets in, she points next to her. "Come on."

I'm already sitting on the bed, so I twist around and get under her comforter. She wraps an arm around my waist, positioning us so I'm the little spoon. Interlacing our fingers at my middle, she leans close to my ear.

"Do you trust me?" she asks in a soft voice, squeezing me to her.

"With my whole heart," I respond immediately.

Her warm breath caresses my ear. "Then let me make you feel good."

I'd do just about anything if she says it like that. That's for sure. And it's not a hardship to allow her to give me pleasure. So I let my tears air-dry and keep myself in the moment as she traces a path down my torso and between my legs with her fingers.

There, she easily slips between my folds. When my legs

jump, she knows she's found the right spot. With the hand of the arm under me, she massages my breast and tweaks my nipple. Kissing the back of my neck and down my shoulder, she rubs my clit until, mere moments later, I relax and my thighs begin to quiver.

Then, what seems like mere moments after that, as I writhe against her bare front, I climax on her finger, in her arms, and in her bed. I thought I was wet before; now, my orgasm drips down the front of my leg. I shudder through my release, warm and safe with her. The rush of it all washes over me soon after, and as she brings her hand back up to hold me tight against her, the intense joy of the moment is way too much. As it finally settles, I'm helplessly thrust into a deep, peaceful sleep.

CHAPTER 5

Patti

That feeling when you wake up next to the person you love is glorious. That permagrin on your lips takes your whole face over when you roll over and pull them close to you. That deep sigh you release once you're tightly snuggled together is one of pure joy. And that totally relaxed state washes over you, threatens to put you right back to sleep because you're so content and happy.

At least, that's what I assume it's like to wake up next to the person you love. Unfortunately, I have no idea. That hasn't happened to me. This morning, I woke up alone, the bed cold like she hadn't been there at all. I want to be frustrated and upset, but this made for no awkward goodbyes. There was no time for false promises or platitudes no one would keep.

Instead, there was just loneliness. Sneaking out. A little pretending like we didn't make out and see each other naked. Like I didn't make her come with my fingers. But whatever.

On my way to work, I stop for coffee. It's the only thing that gets me through a boring day at the office. Especially on a Saturday. And I always stop at the same place, The Steam Room, because they know exactly how I like my coffee by now. I don't have go through the instructions or do it myself, which sounds lazy, but I'm all about what makes my life easier.

Kimber, the cute, blond barista here, definitely makes my life easier.

"Morning," she says cheerily, smiling as I approach the register. "I figured you'd be in soon." She reaches across the counter and palms a to-go cup before lifting it in my direction.

"You are a peach." I give her a wide grin—well, as wide as I can for how emotionally run-down I feel. Then I lean against the counter, retrieving my wallet from my purse. "What in the world would I do without you?"

"Oh, show up to work late. Probably sleep through your workday. Get fired. End up homeless." She winks at me as she takes ten-dollar bill. "I'm a lifesaver, really."

I take my change and my coffee and then stuff a few bucks in the tip jar. "Thank you for literally saving my entire life," I tell her sweetly before turning around and taking a sip of my drink. So. Damn. Perfect.

In the ecstasy of the moment, I close my eyes and then almost run right into someone. I manage to open my eyes just before we smash into each other. But I'm the only one trying to move out of the way. Zo is fixed to her spot, her feet stuck to the floor. And she's staring me down, giving me a look that should have already struck me dead.

"Good morning," I say. It came out a little sharper than I'd intended, but so be it.

I didn't get to say it earlier. She left before I'd even opened my eyes, so I'm not exactly thrilled with her at the moment. And I'm not sure why she is the one who looks like I left her.

With daggers shooting from her eyes, she crosses her arms over her chest. "It certainly seems like you're having a good morning."

"Oh, I'm sorry," I spit back at her, utterly confused. "I'm not the one who crept out of my bedroom this morning before you—"

She flies forward and covers my mouth with her hand. "Shh!"

I steady my coffee so it doesn't spill. Then I dodge her hand and head toward the door. "Thanks again, Kimber," I call over my shoulder. "See you Monday!"

I'm not sorry about not wanting to play her "now you have me, now you don't" game. She wanted that one night; I gave it to her. But, now, I want to move forward and pick the crushed bits of my heart up. If she has no intention of giving me forever, then I have to get past this. I knew that it would come to that, and maybe I was in denial, a little delusional for even admitting it to her. Here we are though. I have choices to make, and not playing into her game is one.

Kimber's loud voice rings out through the coffee shop. "I'll see you, Patti! Have a good day at work."

As I wave back at her and exit the shop, a man in a suit brushes past me. "Goddammit, Chaz. Answer me," he grumbles to his phone.

"Calm down, dude," I mumble under my breath, but he's so engrossed in his phone that he doesn't hear me. Or he ignores me. Whatever.

"Don't tell me to calm down," Zo seethes behind me in a whisper-shout. "And don't call me dude!"

"I wasn't even talking to you," I clarify, stalking toward my car.

"Oh." The sound of her footsteps stops. Then they pick up quickly. "Well, don't walk away from me!"

At that, I halt and spin around. "This is not me walking away from you. This is you walked away from me after I told you I love you and had you naked, in my bed, all night long." I point a finger at her. "If you don't want people to know you did that, you shouldn't have done it. I'm not ashamed of having been with you."

Her eyes go wide and she gazes around the empty

sidewalk to make sure no one else heard that. Then she looks at me again, hooking her thumb toward the coffee shop. "Is she next?"

Now, my eyes mirror hers. "Excuse me?" I put my free hand on my hip.

"You were clearly flirting with her in front of me," she explains.

I shake my head. "Nope. I'm not doing this with you."

"But you—"

"No," I say over her, still shaking my head. "Absolutely not. First of all, I didn't even know you were there. Second, you heard what I said to you the other night and you acted on it. I was selfish and took the one night you were offering me, but that's where this ends, isn't it? I've put my heart through years of this shit, Zo. It has to stop."

I'm sure the use of her real name tells her exactly how serious I am. It certainly seems like it, seeing as her right eye builds a tear. But then her left one does too, and I realize I've hurt her. Which is the last thing in the world I wanted to do, but I react in kind too often. She hurt me, so I've ended up doing the same to her. I've been comforting her and fixing her hurt for half of our lives, so my gut reaction is to do that now. But I can't.

At some point, I have to start comforting myself and fixing my own hurt. Last night may have cost me my best friend, so I guess I'll start with now.

"See you around," I tell her, lifting my coffee in her direction before taking off to my car.

This workday is going to suck ass. This whole weekend might. Or, quite possibly, it could last the rest of my life. Fuck.

***

39

Zo

I shouldn't have left. I know that. I knew it as I was doing it. But hell. If I hadn't left, I would have stayed forever. And the only thing I could think about was losing my parents. The loss of two people is greater than the loss of one, even if that one person could bring me the most happiness I've ever known.

Some might ask why I'd want people who wouldn't unconditionally love me in my life. But they're my parents. They gave me life. How shitty would it be to turn around and completely disappoint them? On the flip side of that coin, how shitty would it be to repress a huge part of me for the rest of my life? Honestly, I don't know which one is worse right now.

Except that maybe I do. As I watch Patti walk away from me, I feel my heart go with her. It beats right out of my chest and leaves a sad trail behind her feet as she goes. Because last night was over way too quickly, but it's the most peace and joy I've felt in a long time. I've never been freer than I was with her. If I could bottle it up, I would. But I was born into the wrong family to ever have that with her permanently.

And what did I do instead? I basically called her a slut and accused her of already "moving on" from something that never really was in the first place. She's free to do as she wants. I'm just so messed up from all of this. And, normally, I'd go to my best friend for advice. Obviously, that's not an option at the moment. I've royally fucked this all up.

I went to The Steam Room to get my favorite breakfast—a lemon poppy seed muffin—but I'm not even close to hungry now. The hunger pains have morphed into knots of nausea. So I go home, call in sick to work, and hide under my covers, praying that all of this blows over and goes away on its own.

Yeah, right. That's wishful thinking at best. But it's all I have right now.

~~~

When Monday morning rolls around, I pick my cell phone up off my nightstand and pull up the contact for work. I've done nothing all weekend, and I'm actually starting to feel like I have the flu. Could just be the power of my thoughts, but I don't want to get anyone else sick, either. Just before I hit the call button, though, my doorbell rings.

I drag my sleepy, probably smell butt to the door, and a peek through the peephole has my heart racing like it's being chased by zombies. But it a better way. I think.

"Open the door, Zed. I know you're right there. And you're not calling in sick to work again."

I can't decide what to do—run away and hide sounds good to my brain. My arm, however, decides for me when it reaches my hand out to swing the door open. It could have, at the very least, checked my hair. But, given that I'm in the clothes she saw me in on Saturday morning, my hair is probably the least of my worries. Good call, arm. Well played.

"Oh, girl," Patti says when she gets an eyeful of depressed me. She, on the other hand, looks as perfect as perfect can be. As always. Her makeup is on point. Her dark bob flows in gorgeous waves. And her clothes are the icing on the perfection cake.

I just turn my back to her and let her follow me in. If she wants to be around an unshowered, messy slob like me, cool. But I wouldn't blame her if she didn't, especially considering how awfully I treated her the other day.

I drop onto my couch and snag the blanket from the back. The least I can do is cover myself up. And acknowledge the fact that I'll forever be a hot mess. This couch could accept me as its own and I'd be happier. Maybe. I don't know.

While I curl up on one side, she sits on the other. Then I notice the paper bag from The Steam Room in her hands.

I want to cry from relief—sustenance has arrived! But…it's from The Steam Room. Which means she likely saw—and flirted with—that barista again. Ugh! How do I turn my brain off?

"Which is first: food or a shower?" Patti asks. "You clearly appear to be in desperate need of both."

"Food," I mumble into the blanket. I can't do much in the shower if I don't have the necessary energy to clean myself.

She opens the bag and digs inside. When her hand emerges, she has my favorite—a lemon poppy seed muffin. The same one I wanted Saturday morning but never got. I must have lived off those alone while I was working and going to dental school. And it's just the thing I need right now.

I gratefully—though hesitantly—accept it from her. As I carefully unwrap the muffin, I sneak a glance at her from the corner of my eye. "Why are you being so nice to me?" I ask her before I take a small bite of yummy muffin goodness.

She sighs. It's short but loud. Then she shrugs. "What are best friends for?"

"Patti, I—"

"We don't have to go there, okay?" She sits back on the couch and peeks inside the paper bag. While pulling her croissant out, she says, "I just missed you, so forget about it." Staring straight ahead, she bites into her bread.

"That's hardly even considered breakfast," I mutter, giving her a hard time and taking the olive branch she's extending me.

We both smirk a little.

Around a mouthful, she says, "It is most definitely considered breakfast in France."

I sweep an arm out around the room. "Does this place look like France to you?"

She laughs, bringing a hand up to her mouth to avoid spitting her food out. "Well, no. Not in the least," she says.

Then she gets more serious. "But I don't need to be in France to eat whatever I want for breakfast."

The look on her face—one raised eyebrow, a half smirk—makes me choke on a piece of muffin, and I bang on my chest as I cough into my hand with the muffin. Apparently, she's not giving up. And, apparently, I like that. Even if it makes everything so much more complicated than it needs to be. Why can't we just be best friends who love each other but can never be together again?

She rubs my back to help settle me down. As she does, I peek at her. She's still perfect-looking. Not a hair out of place. Her red lips draw me in like a moth to a flame. Literally. My face is getting closer and closer to hers, and it's like I have no control. I can't stop it. The only way to stop is to meet her lips with mine. This is how we end up kissing again, muffins and croissants forgotten.

The hand she has on my back presses me closer to her. Her other one cups my cheek and slides into my hair. When I moan against her lips, she sighs into my mouth and our tongues tangle together. I let the blanket fall away so don't have that between us, but the memories of this weekend won't fade as quickly. So I try to back away.

"We shouldn't do this," I whisper, my forehead resting on hers.

"Tell me why," she insists. "One good reason that doesn't include your parents."

I open my mouth to answer, but I have nothing. Beyond my family, it's all fear and worry. Conjecture and speculation. Being different in a world that makes it hard. Coming out as a liar and a fake after so long. But none of that truly matters if I have Patti in my corner. By my side through it all.

So I shake my head.

"That's what I thought," she says. Then she kisses me again, reaching for the hem of my shirt as heat rushes through my veins in anticipation of what's to come next.

CHAPTER 6

Patti

Why can't I stay away? Why do I love this woman so much that she can leave my house after we were first intimate and then insult my very being and I still come back? Well, I don't believe she meant to insult me, for starters. I understand how confused she must be. It's not easy to figure yourself out in this culture. So I get it. But that doesn't mean I have to put up with her hot-and-cold shit. Yet I'm just selfish enough to take what I can get from her. Obviously, it's not doing us any good. Though her being pressed against me feels damn good.

"What about work?" she pants out between kisses.

"We can both be late," I answer, helping her out of her shirt—the same one she was wearing two days ago when I saw her last. Then I stand up and hold a hand out to her. "But I'll help you get there. Come on."

She takes my hand, so I tug her up and right back to me. Once she's in my arms again, she loops hers around my neck as mine go around her back and straight to her bra. I unhook it, wondering why she'd stay in this all weekend. How damn uncomfortable. But that's my proper Zo. Always following the rules. Until now. Thank goodness.

God, her breasts. They're so perfect. Even though I've

seen them a few times in the past—best friends change clothes in front of each other—I never wanted to break her trust or come off as "creepy." So I'm only now realizing how amazing they really are. Just the right size. So soft and perky. I want to worship at their altar for the rest of our lives. If only she'll let me, I will.

I back us down the hall, gripping her hips to guide her. She follows me, her eyes closed as she kisses my lips. Then her hands travel down my shoulders and my arms to the buttons of my shirt. One by one, she undoes them until we're in her bathroom, where she's going to wash away the sadness from the weekend in the shower. With me.

I turn her shower on, adjusting the knob until the temperature will be just right. Once I'm back to her, she pulls my shirt down my arms and swiftly unhooks my bra. The straps fall off my shoulders, and I shrug it off so it drops to the ground between us, joining my shirt. Her hands fly to my breasts like she's never seen them before. Or anyone else's besides her own. Perhaps she hasn't, but that doesn't stop me loving the appreciation she seems to have for them.

When she looks up at me through her thick eyelashes, curiosity shines from her eyes. I give her a barely perceptible nod so she feels comfortable to do whatever she wants. She slowly dips her head toward my chest, and upon reaching it, she reaches her tongue out and swipes it over one of my nipples. To encourage her, I bring a hand to the back of her head and moan. Then she latches on and sucks and I moan some more.

Her lips and her tongue on me are a dream come true. Everything about being with her is more amazing than I hoped it would be. Which makes it that much harder to have to walk away, but for now, I can't help myself. Somehow, though, I pry her away so we can get her cleaned up.

Her pout is absolutely adorable, but she doesn't need to

worry that this is over. I have every intention of seeing this through. But she has to get under the spray with me. Maybe this is an evil plan, but I hope to get so far under her skin, so deep inside her heart, that she'll be willing to put everything on the line to be with me. I'll always be here for her, and maybe, if she knows that, she'll be less scared to fall.

I feel the water, and the temperature is perfect. When I turn back to her, she's right here. As I pull her pants down, I admire her thighs, her knees, and her calves—even with a few days' worth of hair growth. No matter what, she'll always be flawless to me. But she steps out of her pants, farther than she needs to, hiding one leg behind the other like she doesn't want me to see her that way. So I grab her ankle and bring her closer, shaking my head.

"You have nothing to be worried about with me," I tell her as I rise to my full height.

At that, her hands fly to my black work slacks. She undoes the clasp, lowers the zipper, and hooks her thumbs into my panties. Once they're on the floor, she takes her time coming back up my legs. I bite my lip when she pauses near my pussy, rubbing it lightly with the pads of her thumbs. That's more than I can take though.

"Let's get you cleaned up, dirty girl," I say, lifting her by her elbows.

Again, she pouts. "But you said—"

"I know what I said, Zed. But, if we don't get in the shower now, we never will." I give her my best sexy smirk to drive the point home. Then I run a hand through her red locks. "And someone I know desperately needs to wash her hair."

Luckily, she laughs before peeling the shower curtain back so we can step inside the tub. "Okay, bossy." Her smile lights my heart up as she passes me to get under the spray.

Rolling my eyes, I spin around to join her and grin.

That's my girl. No worries, just us being together.

When I get in there with her, she's already drenched. Her eyes close as she soaks her red hair, and water splashes and drips all down her gorgeous body. God, if I thought she was amazing normally, wet-in-the-shower Zo takes my breath away and stops my heart. And makes my jaw fall wide open if the way she has to close it for me is anything to go by.

I blink a few times to focus again and snatch her hand from under my chin. As I press a kiss to it, she blushes and pivots to turn away. But I hold her still.

"Don't. Don't be shy with me. No worries, remember?" I plead with her.

She faces me again and nods. "It's still strange, but it also feels so…"

"So what?" I ask, tucking some hair behind her ear.

"So…" After a deep breath, she rushes out with, "So right."

Yes. She's one hundred percent correct. Everything feels right with when we're together. Like right now. So I lean in and kiss her sweet lips to seal this moment in my memory. Then I reach for her shampoo, squeeze some onto my palm, and lather it up.

As I wash her hair, her eyes flutter closed and she relaxes. Her shoulders fall—along with a small moan out of her mouth. I massage her scalp with my fingers, watching her loosen up more with every passing second. Once her hair is lathered, I guide her head back into the spray and help her rinse the suds out. When that's done, I locate the bottle of conditioner and work that into her hair next.

"God, that feels good," she groans as I coat her hair.

"You know what feels even better?" I say just inches from her face.

Her eyes pop open, and then she purses her lips to the right side of her face. "Well, you grabbed the deep conditioner that needs to sit for a while…"

A slow, naughty smile spreads across my face, and then hers follows. So I drop to my knees, intending to show her exactly what feels better than a head massage. Granted, I've had practice with this. I haven't limited myself when it comes to sexuality just because the woman I love hasn't been available to me. But she's hands down the absolute only one I've wanted to do this to. And, after one swipe of my tongue, I know why. She tastes and smells like sweet heaven and pleasurable hell all wrapped up in one. One taste and I'm already a junkie for her. Just like I thought I would be.

I grip her hips to keep us both steady as I lick between her folds and find her clit. When I hit it, her thigh muscles jump. She lets her head fall back, but her hair ends up in the water, so I turn her until her back is against the wall. Then I raise one of her legs so her foot rests on the lip of the tub and I can see and taste more of her.

From her opening to her clit, I lick. Then I flick her clit over and over with the stiff tip of my tongue. As the pleasure increases for her, her hand goes into my hair, where she presses me closer to her core. I look up at her to get a good eyeful of how gorgeous she is in the throes of passion and I'm nearly brought to tears. But this isn't about me and how much I love this woman right now. This is about her and how good I can make her feel. Because, if I make her feel better than anyone's ever made her feel, I can somehow win this. Win her.

Her head is thrown back and tilted to the side. Her eyes are closed. A small smile builds on her lips, and her tongue is peeking out of her mouth as she bites it. Then her moans become high-pitched pants and her thighs quiver with her impending release. I decide to take a risk and add a finger to the party, sliding it around the rim of her opening. And that does it. A few circles there and a few more clit nibbles and she's falling apart against my mouth.

With one hand still in my hair, she reaches the other out

to the wall next to her, trying to steady herself. So I hold her tighter in my grasp and lazily lick her as she rides her release out. Right until the final twitch and quiver, when she relaxes against the wall and attempts to catch her breath.

As I rise, she lets my hair go, but her hand slides over my shoulder and then down my breast, where she gently squeezes me as though to remember I'm not some man she's with. It's me. Her best friend. The woman who loves her. And, for a moment, I'm worried she's forgotten, but when she opens her eyes, she smiles. Leans forward, wraps her arms around my neck, and kisses me.

Her lips stroke mine as she releases a deep sigh and whispers, "That did feel even better."

That confirmation combined with the way our nipples brush together has electric lust shooting through my veins. The only thing I want to do is ravish her, make her come a million more times just like that. Pushing her before she's ready, though, won't do either of us any good. And I don't even know if she'll ever be ready, but that would send her over the edge. One step at a time.

So I kiss her back and say, "I told you." Then I wink and guide her back to the water to finish rinsing her hair. And hope like hell she'll let me do that again. And again. For, perhaps, the rest of our lives.

***

Zo

It took everything I had to towel off, get dressed, and leave for work. Everything I had not to drop the towel, get in bed, and let Patti do that stuff with her tongue again. My goodness, that was the best thing that's ever happened to me in that shower. And I'll be damned if that never happens again. I just can't seem to wrap my mind around how to make that happen again without hurting the people I love the most. Besides Patti, of course.

Patti. My best friend. Who's now seen me naked, made me come twice, and had her tongue in places no one's ever had their tongue. It should be weird. I've known her forever, but that what makes it easier with her. That's part of why I like her so much. We work so well together. We get along great. And I've said and done some really mean, stupid stuff. But she's still here. Still pursuing this. Still giving me the time of day when I don't deserve it. When we both know how this is going to end.

We've let it sit since that day at my house. It's now Thursday, and I'm trying to get ready to go out with my girls for the night. But I'll see Patti, so I'm having a hard time picking out what to wear. Normally, I'd call her for this kind of thing. Obviously, there's nothing normal about our situation, so I'm not calling her. I entertain the idea of calling Shiree or Lyra, but doing that would raise questions I don't want to deal with. I finally settle on a dress shorter than normal and hope she notices.

"Nice dress," she whispers in my ear the second we're alone enough for her to say that kind of thing to me.

Immediately, my skin flushes red hot. Yes, my actions have received the desired outcome, but I didn't think she'd be so bold as to tell me while we're out with the girls. We've been trying to pry information from Shiree all night, so we haven't had a moment to ourselves. But she's currently headed for the door, so Patti jumped on the opportunity. I, however, need to focus on my friend.

"Shiree! Where are you going?" I shout to her back.

Once we're all outside Lyra's car, she slightly slurs during her explanation. "We don't have to go anywhere, but if I'm going to tell you everything, then we can't be in the bar. No one can hear me. So get in."

The first one to move is Patti. She gets into the back seat, and I join her back there so Lyra can be behind the wheel of her own car. Once we've heard the whole tale about a fake-but-not-really-fake engagement, their definitely real relationship, and more details about their sex life than any of us needed, we decide to go back to Lyra's house to mellow the night out and spend some girl time together.

Together, Patti and I nod and say, "Sounds like a plan!" Then we look at each other.

She's raising her eyebrow at me. Just one. It telegraphs a "way to keep avoiding me" message, because she understood how I said what we said. Whereas I am barely peeking at her because I know why she said it too.

While she simply wants to be there for her friend, I'm using this as an excuse to avoid. Avoidance is the name of my game right now. And I'll take this opportunity and run with it. I don't even know why, exactly. Because I wanted Patti to notice my dress, but I still don't want to face what's happening with us. Facing it makes it real, and I'll worry less if it's not so real in my head right now.

The other two ignore the whole thing and plow on. Then Patti and I agree to go to her fake-but-real engagement party tomorrow. She's our great friend, and she deserves our presence, even if it means missing Friday dinner. My parents will understand this. Though they won't understand other things about me, they'll get this just fine.

At Lyra's apartment, we have some wine. I don't dare drink too much. Lips get loose when too much alcohol is involved. But Patti, in true Patti form, doesn't seem too concerned. I have to step in, though, when we're trading stories and too much information almost leaves her mouth.

"Oh yeah!" she says, her wine sloshing around in her cup. "There was this time when I told this girl I loved her and she kissed me like—"

"I'm ready for bed!" I say way too loudly to cut her off.

"Wait!" Shiree whines at me. To Patti, she conspiratorially asks, "You love someone?"

"Tell us more!" Lyra exclaims, waving her just-painted

nails in the air to dry.

To stop her from saying anything else, I grab her by her shirt and lie through my teeth. "We have early days tomorrow, don't we? I have to get to the office at eight. What time do you need to be at work?"

"You have tomorrow off—" she starts.

"No! I think…" Oh crap. *Think!* "I think we need to check my schedule again. And we should probably all go to sleep." I stand up, dragging Patti with me. "Goodnight!" Then I rush us off to Lyra's spare bedroom.

There, Patti rounds on me. "Oh, lighten up, Zed. I wasn't going to tell them anything."

"I don't care what you were or weren't going to tell them," I tell her, my heart pounding and my blood rushing around my body so fast that I think I might pass out. "You're drunk and don't know what you're saying."

"I don't know what I'm saying?" she spits out. "I don't know that I told you how I feel about you? I don't know that you kissed me like it made your damn life? I don't know that I had my tongue in your—"

"Enough!" I whisper-shout to get her to stop. Mostly because her words are turning me on, and that's the last thing I need right now. "I know you know, okay? We both know!"

"Then what the fuck?" With a hand on her hip, she pops an eyebrow up.

"You know what," is all I say as I avoid eye contact.

"No. No, I don't know what." She throws some pillows off the bed. "And I'm tired of not knowing. I'm tired of pretending like something major isn't happening here."

I sigh and pinch the bridge of my nose. "Seriously. We're not doing this while you're drunk again."

"While I'm 'drunk again,'" she says, using air quotes, "is the only time I'm going to feel like I can call the shots. Take your dress off and get in bed."

"That's so not a good id—"

She crosses her arms over her chest. "Do you trust me?"

I drop my shoulders. She knows the answer to that. I always will.

Her gaze pointedly flicks to my body and then the bed. Even though I huff a breath out, I follow her command. We're at our friend's apartment; she won't do anything crazy here. Not when I'm still so unsure and we're not alone. So I surrender and unzip my dress before getting under the covers. Once she's undressed too, she turns the light off and joins me moments later.

"I'm the little spoon tonight," she states, putting her back to me and grabbing my arm to throw over her middle.

Once she's settled, I tug her closer. She pulls the blanket up around us, and then we relax into a comfortable position. Her dark hair tickles my nose as I breathe her in—sunshine and lemon, her normal scent. I haven't noticed how much I'm addicted to it until this very second though. How much I always think of her when I smell something lemon. How much I love lemon poppy seed muffins because of her. Goodness—has my whole life centered around this woman? At least the last fourteen years have.

"You don't love this like I do?" she asks, a slight shake in her voice. She might have been able to hide it from someone who doesn't know her like I do, but she didn't hide it from me.

Luckily, we're lying on our right sides. So, when my eye starts to tear up, the pillow catches the moisture before it can roll down my cheek.

I grip her hand and link our fingers together. "You know I do," I softly and quietly admit.

"Then why aren't you giving this a serious shot?"

On an exhale, I rush my words out. "Patti, you know exactly why—" But they still don't come out before she shoots my bullshit excuse down.

"Your parents. I get it." She scoots around on the bed

to snuggle deeper into her pillow, her frustration radiating from her. "I just think we're worth the risk. You, Zed, are worth fighting for."

I squeeze her fingers so she knows I heard her, but I have nothing to say. No words will ever convey how much I agree but how little I can do about it. Nothing I can say will stop my heart from racing, my brow from sweating, or my tears from dripping. I'm scared to death of all of it, and the coward part of me wishes it'd all go away. That it hadn't started in the first place. Maybe even that I were normal and hadn't fallen for my best friend, who happens to be another woman.

But none of that can come true. It happened. I fell. And I'll lose everything I've ever known if anyone else finds out. Nothing, not even the promise of sleeping like this every night, makes the idea of telling my parents not terrifying. And, as Patti's breathing evens out and she falls asleep, I worry myself into fitful dreams of complete darkness and being lonely and alone forever.

CHAPTER 7

Zo

When I wake up the next morning, I realize I must have finally hit a deep sleep. The sun is up, my pillow is covered in drool, and dark hair is fanned all over my chest. Dark hair that smells like lemon and sunshine when I take a deep breath of her. Then I remember we're at Lyra's place and I startle.

"Relax, Zed. They're already gone," Patti reasons, holding me in place with her arm around my middle. "I heard them leave for work a long-ass time ago. And I called in sick to work."

I still scoot out from under her and sit up against the headboard, rubbing my eyes. "Why didn't you wake me up?"

Propping herself on her elbow, she says, "Because you don't have to work today and I wanted to spend more time with you like that. So sue me." The smirk she gives me kills any comeback I might have had.

I can't help but give her a small one back. She knows my work schedule and wants to be with me. It's so cute that my heart about bursts.

But then my smirk drops off my lips. "We can't keep doing this."

"And I can't keep telling you that we can," she tells me,

picking at the blanket, her gaze on her fingers. "Because we can—you don't seem to think it's worth it."

Shaking my head, I say, "I've already told you."

She pinches the bridge of her nose and sighs. "This is so not how I wanted to start this day." Then she sits up, folding her legs in front of her. "Look. I've already told you that I love you. You've made it pretty clear that you've at least thought about loving me. And I get that your parents will be upset that you're pursuing a relationship with a woman." She takes my hand in hers and links our fingers. "But I'm not just any woman. Your parents love me. They trust me and know me. And I'll be right there by your side, next to you, when we tell them. Together."

I squeeze her fingers, but it's more because my heart is racing and the room is starting to spin. Shutting my eyes, I attempt to take steady breaths, but the focus on my breathing is actually making things worse. Too much air enters my lungs and not only does the room spin faster, but I'm lightheaded now. So I bend my legs and bring them in close to my body to hug them tight to me, which means letting Patti's hand go. Which also means she notices how badly I'm freaking out.

"Hey," she coos, sitting next to me and putting an arm around my shoulder. "I didn't mean to hurt you."

"You didn't," I say between panting breaths, but that's all I can say before I break down into tears. I put my head on my knees and cry.

"What's going on?" Patti squeezes me to her. "Come back to now, Zed."

But it's too late. Not another one... I can't breathe anymore. I'm about to pass out, I want to crawl out of my skin, and my heart is about to pound right out of my chest. Honestly, I think I'm dying. This might be it. And, even though it's fucking terrifying, if I'm about to die, this is the only place I want to be. Right here in Patti's arms. In fact, the last act of my life will be the truest one of all.

I raise my head and take her lips with mine. They're wet from tears, and the kiss is frantic because I can't breathe, but it's my favorite one yet. It's raw and real, full of everything I feel for this woman. It's passionate, all lips and tongue, hands everywhere they can possibly go. It drives me to stretch my legs out then get onto my knees and straddle her to take this kiss deeper.

As I cup her face and sweep my tongue inside her mouth, she grips my waist and digs her fingers into my hips. I think back to what she said to me yesterday, that I should do whatever feels right. Right now, I feel like letting loose and riding her, so I do. I grind against her for some friction on my clit as I unhook my bra. That spurs her to do the same, and soon, our naked breasts brush against each other in delicious contact.

We've been naked together before, but when she inches her hands down to remove my panties, it feels like the first time. Like this time is going to be the best we've had. And I'm right. As soon as our panties are gone, we return to each other and her thumb goes straight to my clit. At the same time, she sucks one of my nipples into her mouth and nibbles. A moan falls from my lips, and one of my hands goes into her hair as the other one presses behind me on the bed to hold me up.

As much as I love this, we've already done this stuff. I'm ready for more—so much more—when it comes to Patti. So I let her know.

"I want your fingers inside me," I tell her near her ear.

Her finger on my clit stills and her lips pop off my nipple. Then she looks at me. Nods. And lays me down, trailing kisses over my breasts. While kissing up my neck, she spreads me open, rubs her fingers down my slit, and slides one finger around the rim of my opening.

"So wet," she groans, her lips brushing my ear. She gently bites my earlobe before sucking on it.

And then a finger slips inside me. Three swipes of my

G-spot later and I'm coming on her hand, my body so oversensitive that that's all it takes. I shudder through an intense, earth-shattering orgasm that reminds me that I didn't die. I'm still here. With my girl. That relief makes me feel more alive than I've ever felt. And I realize that's how I always feel with her. Nervous and worried as hell otherwise, but with Patti, I'm exhilarated. Buzzing and teeming with life. Not just because I'm with her. Because of her.

This gives me the confidence to scoot back so her fingers leave me and rise to crawl up over her. When our gazes meet, there's a fire in her eyes. A possessive spark full of surprised shock that I'm now taking control. But, considering I thought I was about to die, anything after this moment is a bonus, and I'm going to take full advantage of it.

I pull her down the bed with me so she can lie flat. As I hover over her, I bring my lips down and kiss her while she holds my waist. Her hands glide up my back to press me closer to her, and I move down her body, kissing over her collarbone and all around her breasts until I reach the apex of her thighs. When I place a kiss there, she lets her legs fall open, props herself up on her elbows, and watches me.

Shyness should take over. I should shut down and worry about doing something I've never done all wrong. But I don't. Patti's gaze on me gives me all the confidence I need to spread her open and dip my tongue inside. And holy shit. Her sweet, tangy flavor explodes on my taste buds, and I dive right back in for more. Getting comfortable, I swipe my tongue through her folds, flatten it out, and really explore. She keeps her gaze on me until the tip of my tongue finds her clit. Then she throws her head back and moans.

"Right there," she tells me as I grip her under her backside with my free hand. "Keep going."

Her encouragement spurs me on. I flick it, suck on it, lick it, and swirl around it. When she arches her back, I even nibble on it a little. But then one of her hands slides over my head and holds me there, so I stiffen my tongue and find a steady rhythm to satisfy my girl. Which I do, thank you very much.

With a tight tug on my hair, she finds her release, and I seal my mouth over her to help her ride it out. Ride it out, she does—grinding against my face and moaning as her thighs quiver and her climax soars through her body.

Once she relaxes back onto the bed, I kiss the insides of her thighs and then work my way up. Gentle, soft kisses over her hip and on her side, where she has to stop me as she squirms and giggles.

"Oh, that's right. You're ticklish there," I say, remembering how I figured that out one night during our junior year of high school.

With her head resting on the bed, she turns her gaze down to me, a shy, girly smile on her lips. "Mmhmm."

I kiss her there once more anyway, and she laughs lightly, which is music to my ears. Then I lick a path from her navel to up between her breasts. Moving to the right, I twirl my tongue over her nipple, and a soft, quiet sigh leaves her mouth. When I put my lips on hers, she sweeps her tongue into my mouth, and knowing she can taste herself on me sends a lightning bolt of lust right between my legs.

She hums her approval, her lips curling into a grin against mine. "I never would have guessed you've never done that before."

"Who says I haven't done that before?" I tease.

Pulling away, she stares up at me, raising an eyebrow. Falling onto my side, I dissolve into giggles though, because obviously, I haven't. And she knows that. She knows me better than anyone.

Her eyebrow relaxes. In fact, her whole face settles into a softer expression. "That's the Zed I know and love. The one who laughs, not cries." She rolls onto her side, props herself up on an elbow, and traces her fingers down my rib cage. "What happened back there?"

I almost forgot how awful and scary that felt. Almost. But being with her this way relieves a lot of it. Makes those feelings and that worry fall away.

"Panic attack," I say, looking away from her.

She freezes. "You say that like it's not the first time it's happened."

I suck my bottom lip into my mouth, still not making eye contact with her.

"Zo." She flattens her hand on my side and shakes me. "What's going on?"

"What isn't going on?" I mumble.

Her sigh is long. "This doesn't have to be this complicated. You're going to worry yourself to death if you don't just make a decision. I know exactly how you work, but I had no idea it was this bad. And I wouldn't have pushed it or told you how I felt if—"

I stop her with a kiss. We're at a bit of an awkward angle, but I don't care. I bring my hand to her head and keep her close, sweeping my tongue past her lips to tangle with hers. While we kiss, I realize I need to decide. I wouldn't have anything to decide if she hadn't pushed and told me how she felt. But I'm glad I do. I'm freaking thrilled, actually. Over the moon that, even though this makes me different and it'll be weird for other people, I have a real shot at happiness. This woman and what we have, I now understand, is way more important than fear and worth much more than living without her to please other people.

I've been miserable while trying to push my feelings down and pretend I don't love another woman. But I do. Not any woman. The best one I know. The best one I'll ever know. The one who's been there for me for more than half of my life. The one my parents already know and love. Patti has a point there. So maybe this won't be as bad as I thought.

"Don't say that," I say against her lips. "I'm fine. And I'm even better now that I know that this is real. I've felt crazy for a long time, and yes, I freak out about everything." I tuck some hair behind her ear and then cup her neck. "But all of that melts away with you."

This time, she kisses me. It's short, but our connection is intense. Then she pulls back and looks me dead in the eyes. "What does that mean? You have to spell it out for me. Plain English."

I blink a few times, gathering my thoughts and calming my racing heart. "It means," I say before needing to suck a big breath of air in. "It means I want this. Me and you." A small smile spreads on my lips. "Us." Then I kiss her lips to seal the deal.

***

Patti

Holy hell on wheels. This is happening. It's really fucking happening. The woman of my dreams is kissing me, and she just declared us a couple. Like, a real fucking couple. I don't know what that looks like in the scheme of things, but right now, it looks like the two of us naked, in bed, and epically happy. That's all there is to it, and that's all there needs to be. Just us.

But Zo's cell phone rings in her purse, which is on the chair in the corner. So it looks like this happy bubble isn't going to last all that long.

"It could be work or my parents," she reasons as she scrambles off the bed and goes over to her purse. "Hey. Lyra," she says into the phone, a little out of breath as she peeks back at me. "What's up?"

I'd like to think that was because of me, but it could be from how she kind of rushed to answer the call. Either way, I'm up and standing behind her in seconds. If this is the last of our happy bubble, we'll be skin to skin. That's for sure.

I don't hear what Lyra says, but it doesn't matter. This girl just agreed to be mine, so I wrap my arms around her middle from behind her and rest the side of my head on her shoulder.

"No, not at all," Zo replies. But there's a lot of pep in her voice.

I brush my fingers across the bare skin of her stomach, thinking my touch might relax whatever she's worrying about right now. All it does, though, is make her giggle.

"Stop!" she says around a laugh, swatting at my hand.

This time, I can make part of Lyra's response out. "I'll just call you—"

"No, it's fine!" Zo spins around and out of my grasp. "Seriously," she says to Lyra—though she's looking at me. Then she exits the room and closes the door behind her.

I can't hear the rest of her conversation. But I'm one hundred percent sure she's not telling our friend what just happened in the spare room of her apartment. Nor is it likely she's mentioning that she's not single anymore. Which is something I won't soon let her forget.

Should I get dressed? Or should I wait for her to come back and decide if she wants more? Some things will need to be in her hands. Otherwise, I might scare her off. She already knows how deeply I feel for her, but that doesn't always translate in words. Yes, I used the word love. That was just a week ago though, and this new panic attack thing is enough to make me want her in a bubble where nothing can hurt her or freak her out. Including me.

So I won't push the love issue, but I'm not going to let this hang between us with no forward movement anymore. No, this is happening now. We're both on that page, and we won't go backwards. I won't let us. It's a matter of how far forward she's willing to go. That can make or break us.

She comes back in the room, her phone at her side, and closes the door. It's a lot more silent in here now for some reason. Like the lack of sound sticks out more now that we've been interrupted. And I'd do a lot of bad things to find out what she's thinking right now. But I can't push the woman who breaks down into panic attacks without the fear of hurting her. So I stare at her and wait. She's naked though, so it's not a hardship. Not that it would be if only her eyes were visible, but hey.

When she releases a breath, I expect her to finally speak. And she does. Thank goodness. That silence was getting louder and louder.

"That was Lyra," she says, stating the damn obvious.

"I'm aware," I slowly reply. "Everything okay?"

She nods once. Quickly. "We should find what we're wearing to Shiree's party tonight. I don't think she'll call you, but she wanted to make sure we'll still be there."

"That one loves control," I mumble, rolling my eyes. But I nod at Zo. "Okay. We'll head to the mall. I guess we'll Uber it and then go get your car."

When she swallows, the gulp is audible. "Together?" she questions.

I draw my eyebrows down. "Of course together. We do most things together, don't we?"

Her eyes flash wide before she schools her features. Then a smirk takes her mouth over before she can stop it. I love how her emotions always play out over her face. She can't hide much from me.

"We do a lot more together now," I say, taking the few steps over to her. I snake my arms around her waist and glide my hands down her backside to pull her closer to me. "But let's be open about this with each other. We can take this as fast or as slow as you want—as long as we move forward."

She gulps again, so I run my hands up her back in soothing motions.

"Talk to me."

After a deep breath, she says, "I don't know how fast or

slow I want to take it."

I lean in and rub my nose to hers. "That's okay. Just as long as you're all mine." Then I kiss her perfect mouth. Though I taste her nervousness like it's sour on my tongue. Pulling back, I ask, "You're mine, right?"

Quickly, she nods in small movements. "Yours." Then she gazes down before looking at me again. "And you're mine?"

"One hundred percent," I tell her with no hesitation. "Have been for twelve years."

Again, her eyes widen. They don't return to normal quite as fast as before though.

"Twelve?" she asks, blinking at me, clearly bewildered.

I have to stifle a laugh. "You really had no idea?"

She shakes her head, her nostrils flaring. "No," she finally says. "I thought I was the secret keeper."

This time, I'm unable to keep my laugh under wraps. But it's light. "With everything else, you are." I squeeze her to me and kiss her. "What about you?" I ask. "Not quite as long, I'm sure."

"What makes you say that?" She trails paths on my lower back.

I raise an eyebrow. "You'd have worried yourself straight to your deathbed by now," I deadpan.

A closed-mouth smile curves her lips. "Fair enough." She stares at me for a few moments in silence. Then she says, "You know me so well. But what made you know that now was the right time to tell me?"

I press my lips together and shrug. "Just felt right. Like you might understand if I told you now."

When she doesn't reply, I kiss her forehead, hoping to ease some of the worry I saw creeping into her brow.

"My parents will never understand," she says, her voice shaky.

Pain grips my heart and slashes it in two. My need to put her in that protective bubble rises again. Because the last thing I want to do is come between her and her parents. I love them too. They're like my own parents, given how they've treated me ever since I met them and Zo. But people who can't accept that love doesn't fit into a box have no place in my life. People who can't accept me for who I am don't need to stick around. Having Zo permanently by my side as more than just my friend would more than make up for their loss. I don't expect her to see it that way yet, but I'll do my best to prove to her than I can more than make up for it for her too.

"We don't have to tackle that right now," I reassure her. "One step at a time, okay?"

When she nods her agreement, I kiss her forehead again and rest my lips there.

"Just promise to talk to me when things aren't going how you want them to," I say against her skin. "I can be patient as long as you stick with me. I won't do the back-and-forth we're-together-no-we're-not thing though. You're either in or out. My heart's not strong enough to keep losing you now that I have you."

When I lean back to see how she took that, tears are shining in her eyes. God, I don't mean to keep making her cry, but some things are going to be tough. The only easy part about this relationship is being with each other. We're about to hit a bumpy road, one that might throw us a lot of obstacles we'll have to overcome. But, if we do it together, we'll make it. I need her on that page with me.

After a sniffle, she nods. "I'm gonna need your patience," she says, her voice watery. Backing up, she takes my hands and squeezes them. Then she gives me a look that makes hope soar through my heart.

One that also makes my stomach plummet with worry.

CHAPTER 8

Zo

Together, Patti and I show up at Shiree's fake engagement party. But, as far as everyone else is concerned, we drove here together. That's all. Just like we normally would have. Everything is normal. Nothing's out of the ordinary. Nope. Not a thing.

Well, maybe the feeling in my stomach isn't ordinary. The clenching, the rolling, the churning... I'm Fort Knox with secrets, especially my own. But this one isn't even one I want to keep. Yet it's the one I feel I have to keep the most. The one I have to most strongly guard. Which is the worst kind of contradiction at a party dedicated to love—fake though it may be.

However, when Patti puts her hand on my arm to guide me toward Lyra, my stomach calms. She seems to do that to me, and I'm going to need that now more than ever.

Lyra, though, looks exactly like I feel. And I wonder what secret she's keeping that's making her feel that way.

"I'm so glad you two are here," she stresses when she reaches us. She hugs us both. "You look amazing." Then she turns her attention solely to me. "Especially you."

"Normally, I'd take offense to that," Patti mutters, smiling.

But this isn't a normal situation we find ourselves in, she

doesn't say. And she'd smile wider at that, I bet.

Lyra seems too distracted to really care. "I'm sitting over here." She waves at us to follow her.

At the table, we meet Blake, Chaz's right-hand man. That's only because he introduces himself. Lyra ignores him while we shake hands, and then we fall into an awkward silence. Patti and I exchange a brief there-is-Lyra's-secret look before a man taps on the mic and introduces Mr. Charles Masters and Miss Shiree James to the party.

After Chaz's incredibly well-spoken speech, in which he dropped the bomb that they're actually married and he's stepping down as CEO of his company and appointing Blake as his successor, we watch the happy couple dance. I'm so pleased that my friend has found joy and love. By the way she's smiling and laughing with her new husband, she certainly seems content and blissful. Everyone deserves that. Including me, even if I don't know what that looks like yet.

While at the bar in the ballroom, I can't help the twinge of jealousy that skates down my spine at how open with their love they can be. Earlier today, the happiest moment of my life occurred, but it's all marred by having to keep it a secret. Until when though? We can't do that forever. I certainly don't want to, and Patti won't stand for it. I just can't see the light at the end of this tunnel yet, and I don't know what to do about it. She'll be patient, but for how long? And how long can we go without anyone knowing? Wanting to be free to take my girlfriend for a spin on the dance floor isn't too much to ask, is it?

Girlfriend. How weird is that?

Patti breaks me out of my thoughts when she tells Lyra, "Hey, I think Zed and I are gonna take off now that Shiree's leaving."

In agreement, I nod. "Yeah, I have an early start tomorrow, so I should head out."

Lyra's face falls, but she quickly shifts it to hide her disappointment. "Oh, okay. I should probably go too. If you two aren't here, I don't know anyone else."

"Are you sure about that?" I ask her, peering over her shoulder. "Because it looks like Blake is coming this way."

"Oh, he was just being nosy earlier because I was with Shiree and Chaz," she replies, attempting to dismiss me. "It's nothing."

I don't buy it at all though. And I wonder if she's hiding something just as big as Patti and I are. We've all heard what Blake did to keep Chaz and Shiree apart. Apparently, it didn't work, seeing as they're freaking married now. But it seems as though Lyra knows something we don't. And has feelings she doesn't want to acknowledge.

Wow. That sounds way too familiar.

Patti hugs her and quietly says something in her ear. It's too quiet, so I don't catch it. It does, however, make Lyra's eyebrows rise before her whole brow creases. It isn't my business anyway, so I wait until they're done with their embrace before I move in for one to say my goodbye. Then Patti and I leave the party and head for my car.

"An early start tomorrow?" she asks as soon as we're there.

I unlock the doors. "Yep." Over the top of the car, before I get in, I wink at her. Then I open the door and drop into the driver's seat.

It takes her a few stunned seconds, but then she's next to me in my car, placing her hand on my thigh. As I start the engine, I drop my gaze to her hand. That's exactly where it should be when we're sitting next to each other like this. I know that with every fiber of my being. Nothing about it feels wrong or morally broken, yet every fiber of my being also knows how my parents will feel about this. It'd be a lie to say I'm not scared to death, but I said I'd give this a shot. And the least I can do in private is really give us a chance to see what this is between us. I'm just worried I already know.

"My place or yours?" I ask her, staring straight ahead, my hand on the gear shifter.

Out of the corner of my eye, I see her grin. I think I feel it more than I can see it. It lights the dark car up with its happiness, which is yet another reason why I'm jumping into this with her. She has so much life and presence. Anyone would be a fool to pass up being with her. I can only hope she'll be as patient as I need her to be.

"You pick. Doesn't matter to me as long as we're together."

I look at her, and the truth shines in her eyes. So I say, "We'll go to mine. That way, your car isn't at my place overnight."

That grin slides right off her lips. All of the happiness is sucked out of the car too.

Then I realize what I said and how that came out. So I backpedal. "Sorry. I just meant that... I mean, it wouldn't necessarily be suspicious, but—"

She holds a hand up between us—the one that was on my thigh. After a silent moment, she closes her eyes and says, "I get it, but that doesn't mean that it doesn't hurt. Okay?"

I nod, but when her eyes open, I nod again so she'll see. My right eye must be tearing up, because she brings that raised hand to my face and wipes under my eye with her thumb.

She releases a deep sigh. "We'll figure this out. I promise."

Leaning against her palm, I close my eyes. After a rushed-out exhale, I blink them open, shift into reverse, and start the journey back to my place—wishing with all of my heart that my brain would get on its page.

***

Patti

"Wake up, sleepyhead," I whisper in her ear from my

side of her bed. "Someone promised me an early start to the day."

Maybe it's crazy, but no matter how many times we satisfy each other, it's just not enough. I want more and more, and I'm immediately looking forward to the next time I'll have her naked. Plus, it helps that she's so naturally taken to being intimate with me. There's no real awkwardness or fumbling. It's like the worry center in her brain gets switched off when we're between the sheets. Or in the shower. Or on her couch. Whatever. When we're together, she's a much more easygoing version of herself.

Until she gets in her head, that is. But that's going to happen with her. That's who she is—a worrier to the core. I knew that going in, and I'll figure that out with her as much as I can. Even when it hurts, like her comment in the car last night. I understand how her brain is working right now, so I'll work with it the best I can. It might not seem like the best to her, but that's all I can offer right now.

She stirs when I trail my fingertips over her bare belly. Sleepily, she rolls over to face me, and I kiss her nose.

"There she is," I say, hoping to coax her eyes open.

"What time is it?" she grumbles, her lids staying shut.

"I don't even know, but the sun is out. So it's time to get up."

She still doesn't move, so I roll her over until I'm hovering above her. That pops her eyes wide open.

"Okay, okay," she says around a laugh as I nuzzle against her neck. "Don't even think about it. I'm starving to death, woman."

I raise my head to stare at her. "To death?" I question, one eyebrow up.

"Yes!" she exclaims, smiling and squirming out of my grip. When she's up, she walks her naked body over to her dresser for clothes. As she puts them on, she says, "Someone's sucked all of my energy. All I have left is enough to get dressed."

"Why would you use the last of your energy to put clothes on?" I ask. It's half sarcastic but half totally bewildered-sounding.

"Because I'm freaking hungry and I need to eat!" She flops back on the bed fully clothed, the back of her hand coming to rest on her forehead. "You're going to have to make me breakfast."

So dramatic. But I kind of love it. "Well, you're in luck." I roll out of bed and head for my clothes. "I know a place that already has breakfast ready and waiting for us. My coffee will probably be waiting for me too."

She turns her head—only her head—toward me. "Let me guess. The Steam Room."

Hooking my bra, I say, "Yep!" Then I realize all I have is my dress from last night. So I go to her dresser for a shirt.

"That's right," she drawls. "The place with the flirty and friendly baristas…"

My hands freeze with the shirt I picked halfway over my head. Once I've straightened it out, I hit her with a stare. "Don't even."

She mimes zipping her lips, but I squint at her to drive the point home. It's utterly ridiculous that she thinks I'd leave her for Kimber. Or anyone for that matter. I already told her. I've waited twelve years for this. I wouldn't fuck it up now that I have her.

After borrowing some yoga pants, I get her starving ass out the door. I'm going to have to get home soon so I can get into the office and make up for yesterday, so we kind of have to hurry. That doesn't mean I want to. So I try to savor every quiet, hand-holding second we have together in the car. By the time it's our turn in line, I'm glad I did.

Yes, my coffee is ready and waiting for us. Which isn't a problem—for me, anyway. I said that it might be. But, when I add Zo's lemon poppy seed muffin, Kimber decides to strike up some conversation.

"Trying something new today, Patti?" Kimber asks as

71

she reaches for the muffin.

"It's for my girlfriend," automatically tumbles out of my mouth. Then I freeze.

Look at this logically though. The muffin is for my girlfriend. And I'm damn proud of being with Zo. Even if she's frozen in a wide-eyed stare that's shooing laser beams into the back of my head. I can't see her, but I can damn well feel her.

Kimber must notice too. She flicks her gaze from me to Zo and then back to me. "Oh. I didn't realize you were seeing someone."

I turn my head toward Zo, who is most definitely killing me with lasers. And her chest rapidly rises and falls with her quick breaths. As her expression morphs more into fear rather than anger, I know exactly what's happening. But she rushes out of the coffee shop before I can help her.

I hastily snatch a ten-dollar bill out of my wallet and slide it across the counter. "I am now," I inform Kimber.

She covers my hand with hers. "You might want to tell her that." Then she takes the bill and hands me the bag with Zo's muffin.

I accept the bag and pick my coffee up from the counter. "Keep the change."

When I'm on the sidewalk, I look both ways to find Zo. She's off to the right, toward where she parked her car, squatting on the ground. Hunched over and breathing far too hard. I rush over to her and nearly drop my coffee while attempting to get my arms around her, but that hardly matters. Coffee is replaceable. A worried-to-death Zo is not.

"Hey," I say quietly near her ear. "It's okay. Breathe."

"It's not okay!" she chokes out. When she raises her head, she looks at me with tear-stained cheeks. Sobbing, she falls to the ground on her butt and slumps over almost into a ball.

My heart breaks, though I'm not one hundred percent certain what part isn't okay. Is it not okay that we're together? Is it not okay that she seems ashamed of being with me? Is it not okay that we have to hide this from everyone? Is it not okay that I almost told someone we're together? Is it not okay that I'm so over the moon about being with her that I want to tell everyone? What exactly isn't okay?

She's not up for those questions though. That much I know. I'll ask her when she's calmer. For now, I need to comfort her so I actually still have a girlfriend later.

I join her on the ground and remove her muffin from the bag. I even unwrap it for her and put the garbage back in the bag. Then I slide my free arm around her shoulders, squeeze her to me, and say in a low voice, "Come back to now, Zed." Maybe it's cheating, but I also wave the muffin below her face, hoping the scent wafts up to her nose.

Luckily, it works. She starts to calm down, her shoulders not shuddering with the force of her tears anymore.

"Take a deep breath," I continue to tell her. "In through your nose, out through your mouth."

She does until she can sit all the way up without breaking down again. I bend my left knee and rest my elbow on it, keeping the muffin within her reach so she can take it when she's ready. After a few moments, she does, and I think I see a hint of a smile on her lips. I definitely do when she bites into it.

"I'm a basket case," she says around a mouthful of muffin.

I squeeze her closer. "You can say that again."

She scoffs, but it's all in jest. "You were supposed to tell me I'm not."

"Nope," I say, shaking my head. "'Best friends'"—I use air quotes with my free hand—"tell each other the truth."

When she turns her head fully toward me, confusion is swimming in her gaze. After a deep sigh, she says, "Seriously. I don't know how to do any of this. It's a simple word, but I wasn't expecting it so soon, and I freaked out."

"Well," I say after a single nod, "I think the first step is to get off the dirty sidewalk. That might help."

She softens her facial expression and her rigid posture. "You don't have to pretend like it doesn't bother you."

I give her one last squeeze and rest the side of my head against hers. "I know. One step at a time." Then I let her go and stand up. "But maybe you could not run away," I offer, holding my hand out to help her up.

When her hand lands in mine, it feels like much more than just assistance. The power behind her grip feels more like we're making a deal. A deal to be more of a team on this. To stand stronger in the face of this new situation. We're together. In strength and in reality.

How could that possibly go wrong?

CHAPTER 9

Zo

By some miracle, we've managed alone time for two weeks. Two whole weeks of that new-relationship goodness. That blissful, fun, everything-is-happy-and-good part of the relationship. We've even made it through two Thirsty Thursday nights out with Shiree and Lyra and no one's suspected anything or been weird. And, as far as I'm concerned, there's no end in sight.

Well, except for tonight, maybe. It's the first Friday dinner with my family since Patti and I officially started dating. And, because we missed the one two weeks ago for Shiree's party and last week because my parents were busy, they definitely want us both there. They miss us, they said, and we have to be there at six p.m. sharp.

If it weren't 5:59 and I weren't outside their house, parked behind Patti's car, I probably wouldn't be freaking out as much. But it's 5:59—nope, it's actually six now—and I'm outside their house, parked behind Patti's car. So I'm a bucket of fear and worry. And the bucket is full.

"Zoeybell!" my dad says with enthusiasm as I walk in the door. Then he hugs me tight. "How was work today?"

I practically melt in his embrace. I love my dad, how soft he is with me and kind he is to my mom. And I'm sure he'd love for me to end up with a man just like him. But, when I think about it, Patti's also soft and kind. She's exactly what he wants for me. Just with the wrong parts. And that, to them, makes all the difference. Obviously, I won't be telling them tonight.

"It was fine, Dad." I squeeze him back and then let go to follow him into the kitchen.

My mom's at the stove, pulling a roast out of the oven. "Hi, honey. Glad you made it right on time."

"Smells good, Mom," I say, dropping into the chair next to Patti's.

"Doesn't it?" Patti turns to my mom's back. "You've outdone yourself, Ma. I can't wait to dig in." When she faces me again, she's smiling, her eyes lit up.

"She's been slaving over it for hours," my dad tells us, putting his arm around my mom while she stirs gravy in a pot.

"Oh, it's nothing." She dismisses us with a wave of her hand. "Patti, doll, will you set the table? Zo, want to get the silverware and napkins?"

"Of course," Patti agrees as we both get up from the table.

Five minutes later, the table is set, the food is in the center, and we're all sitting, ready to eat. But, before we do, we all hold hands to prepare to say Grace.

"Honey," my mom says to my father, "will you do the honors tonight?"

He smiles, closes his eyes, and bows his head. So we follow suit. Once he's thanked Our Heavenly Father for all of our blessings and good fortune, we're able to start eating. I, however, want nothing more than to empty my stomach rather than fill it. Nausea builds as my stomach rolls. Bile creeps up my throat. But I force carrots and potatoes down to appear as normal as possible. No one here has secrets. Nope. Not one.

"Zo." My mom's voice catches my attention sometime later. "You're just pushing your food around. Is everything okay?"

Crap. I've been caught. "Oh yeah," I say as cheerily as possible. "Just a long day at work on my feet. Lots of patients. Too many cavities." I smile, though lightly is all I can manage, to throw her off the scent.

After a moment, she relents. "Okay." Then she takes a bite of roast. "Oh. Have you thought any more about getting a dog?"

"I thought it was a cat," my dad chimes in.

"It was a cat," Patti confirms. "Are you thinking about getting a dog now? You didn't tell me that."

"That's because I never said I wanted to get a dog," I immediately reply, but it comes out more harshly that I intended.

Patti isn't pleased with my tone. "Seems like you're not saying a lot of things," she mumbles under her breath. But I caught it.

With wide eyes and a racing heart, I glare at her. What in the ever-loving hell is that about?

"What was that, sweetie?" my mom asks her.

Patti puts her fork in her mouth. Chews. Shakes her head with a too-sweet smile aimed at my mom. When she's swallowed her food, she says, "Nothing. I think a dog would be great. Someone needs to keep our girl company."

My dad laughs. "That's a good point. That house must be lonely without a man there with you. Do you have any dates lined up?"

I gulp and flick my gaze to my dad, pushing my potatoes around on my plate. "No, Dad. None at all."

"Honey, didn't someone new start coming to church last week?" my mom asks him. "What's his name? Darrel?" She turns her attention to me. "We'll find out if he's single for you. Don't worry."

"That's a great idea," Patti agrees, stabbing a carrot with her fork. "Is Darrel cute? Maybe he already has a dog."

I drop my fork onto my plate with a loud clatter.

"Stop!" I shout louder than I needed to. So I quiet my voice. "Sorry. But please. Stop. I'm fine."

"Are you sure?" my mom prods. "You seem rather nervous today, and you've barely eaten a th—"

"Yes! Mom, I'm fine. Okay? I'm fine." I stand up so fast that my chair topples over behind me. After a moment, I right it and tuck it under the table. "Thanks for dinner, but I'm gonna head home now. I'm just tired after a long day. I'll see you guys later."

"Zoeybell," my dad calls after me, but I ignore it.

I shut the door behind me, thankful for the cool evening air. But the door opens and closes when I'm halfway down the driveway on the way to my car.

"What the hell was that?" Patti asks.

When I spin around, she's pointing back at the house. Her face is scrunched, and she's vibrating with frustration.

"Oh, I could say the same to you," I spit back at her as quietly as I can while she's still able to hear me. "What are you mad at? You're the one who almost spilled our secret!"

"That's the whole point," she sneers, crossing her arms over her chest.

When I don't do or say anything, she tosses her arms in the air and then marches over to her car. So I follow.

"You don't get it." She hits the button on her fob to unlock her door.

I stop in front of her. "No, I guess I don't."

"I just thought..." Taking a deep breath, she glances up at the sky. Then she releases the air and looks at me. "It's been a while now. And this was the first dinner we've had with your family since..." She waves a finger between us. "So I thought..."

I blow out a breath, put my hands on my hips, and stare at the ground. She thought I'd already be ready to tell them that their daughter does have dates lined up, but they're with a woman? Oh yeah. A couple of weeks is long enough for me to gather the strength to ruin my parents' lives. Plenty of time.

Actually, the only thing it's long enough for is for me to lose my dinner all over the road next to Patti's car. What little I ate of it, anyway. Luckily, I miss her shoes, but it isn't by much.

Immediately, her hands go to my hair to hold it back as I retch in the street. I think some already made it into my hair though. If it did, she doesn't seem bothered. Instead, she rubs circles on my back.

"Goddammit. I'm sorry, Zed," she says while I spit the rest of the vomit out. "I don't even know what came over me. I had a hard day at work, and then, when you didn't immediately tell them, I just...saw red." She pauses her hand on my back. "It wasn't your fault, and I shouldn't have done that."

When I stand up, her hand falls off me and she lets my hair go. I wipe my mouth with the back of my hand. Then my vision goes black as the world spins around me and I sway right into her arms.

"Whoa!" she says. "I got you." She holds me until I'm able to see again. "Did you just get up too fast?" she asks when I'm standing on my own again.

I nod, rubbing my eyes "Yeah, I think so."

"Well, you just lost the dinner you barely touched too." She puts a hand on her hip. "You should probably eat something. What did you have for lunch?"

Squinting, I think back to lunch. Dr. Phelps ordered pizza for everyone, but I wasn't very hungry when it came in. By the time I was ready to eat, I was busy with back-to-back-to-back patients and never got the chance. And I can't even remember breakfast. I don't want to tell her that though. So I just shrug.

Her eyes widen and then she blinks at me, huffing a breath out of her nose. Then she opens her car door. "Follow me," she says before getting in, shutting the door, and starting her car.

As long as it's away from my parents—and hopefully to food—I'll follow her.

Oh, who am I kidding? I'll follow this woman almost anywhere. Except, apparently, down the path that leads to telling my parents how we feel about each other.

***

Patti

This woman might be the death of me. If stress and worry aren't the death of her first. God. She's so stubborn because she's so scared. And we were so close to telling Lyra at our first Thirsty Thursday night without Shiree—she's on her honeymoon with Chaz. But Lyra has bigger issues of her own to worry about, so Zo clearly didn't want to spill the beans.

Which I get. I understand not wanting to burden a friend while she has a lot going on. But for heaven's sake. When will it be our turn? It's been over a month now, and I've only accidentally told the barista at the coffee shop. All because my girlfriend still needs to keep us a secret. Honestly, I'm not sure how much longer I want to be a secret. It feels dirty. Yet, if it's the only way for me to be with her… I'll take what I can get, I guess.

Not forever though. We can't keep this from everyone we love forever. I won't stand for that, and it'll likely kill Zo in the long run—literally. So I need something from her. Just a little give in my favor. We don't have to tell anyone, but I would like to go out with her. On a real, honest-to-god date.

Don't get me wrong. I love nothing more than the alone time we spend together. It's like heaven when we're wrapped up in each other, bare skin to bare skin, tangled in blankets and bedsheets. Being out with my girl on my arm would be like heaven too though.

And she could at least use it as a means to tell her parents the truth in a roundabout way. That she's seeing someone, going on dates, and starting a relationship. They'll want to meet him, but together, we can come up with ways to get around that. I want her parents to know how happy she is. I want to see them be happy for her. Because, when we do tell them, they will have to see how ridiculous it'd be to be upset just because I'm not a man. Nothing else will have changed about the situation but that.

So I say, "Hey. Let's go to the movies tonight," as we lie in her bed, naked and satisfied, in the middle of the afternoon. I even roll onto my side to face her.

"Okay," she agrees. Too easily. She tucks her hands under the side of her face. "What do you want to see?"

"Doesn't matter." I steal a kiss and tuck some fiery hair behind her ear. "I just want to go out with you."

Her body goes rigid under my touch, but then she blinks and says, "Like a date?"

Slowly, I nod. I don't want her to freak out, but yeah. Exactly like a damn date.

An unhurried smile spreads across her lips. "You want to take me on a date?"

I raise an unamused eyebrow. "Zed. It's been how long now? Don't you think you deserve to be taken out on a date?"

Her smile morphs into a smirk. "Well, yeah." And then it disappears. "But—"

"Nope." I shake my head. "We're allowed to go out. Everyone knows we're best friends. We used to go to the movies together all the time. It's not unheard of, and no one will suspect anything, so stop worrying."

She releases a deep breath. "Fine." Then her smirk is back. "I'd love to go on a date with you."

A grin breaks out over my face now. Until she nearly shoves me out of her bed.

"What the hell was that for?" I question, stumbling off

the mattress and righting myself.

"If you're going to take me out on a date, you're going to do it properly." She gets up off the bed and heads for the door. There, she pauses in the doorframe. "And you know my usual pre-date ritual. So you have to go so I can get ready before dinner with my family tonight." Before she darts down the hall, she gives me a cheesy smile.

One that lands right in my heart and renders me speechless.

I quickly dress as she starts the water in the shower. As I pass the bathroom door, I briefly think about going in there and joining her, but she's right. If we're going to go on a date, we should do it the right way. So I grab my purse on the way out and head home.

Once I'm out of the shower and off the phone with Lyra—she's having more Blake problems, and I might have accidentally admitted that I'm going on a date tonight—I text Zo. I want to know which movie she wants to see, even though I couldn't care in the slightest. I'll sit through whichever romantic comedy fright-fest movie or whatever she wants to see. As long as, in the dark of the theater, I can hold her hand and pretend we're a normal couple.

She doesn't message me back right away, but that's okay. I imagine she's painting her toenails in the middle of her bed like she usually does before dates. I wonder what color she thinks I'm worthy of. Though I'll see soon enough.

~ ~ ~

Purple. She chose purple polish for her toes, which are looking super cute in her open-toe shoes. And that's the first thing I say to her when I'm back at her house to pick her up for Friday dinner.

Her eyes widen as she smiles. Before she speaks, she tames her expression. "Someone once told me that, if my date was smart, they'd notice purple."

My heart thuds in my chest. She remembers that

conversation too.

"What I didn't say that day," I tell her, offering her my arm, which she hesitantly accepts, "is that I told you to go with purple because it's the best color on you. You look great in every shade, but purple…" I whistle a high-to-low tone.

As we walk to my car, she visibly melts a little, apparently pleased with my compliment. I'm glad. She deserves to be complimented and praised. She's beautiful inside and out—even when she insists on hiding us. Hiding me.

When we get to the passenger's side of my car, I open the door. She gets in, and I close it before walking around to the driver's side. As I start the car, she turns her body to face me.

"My favorite color on you is light blue," she informs me. "I think it brings out the brown of your eyes."

"Duly noted." I wink at her and drive us to her parents' house.

The whole way there, she holds my hand. Even as I park my car on the curb. When we've both unbuckled our seat belts and it's time to get out of the car, she takes a deep breath and squeezes my fingers. So I don't move. I wait for whatever she has to say.

"I'm sorry I don't want to tell them yet," she says, looking at our entangled fingers. "But I almost told Lyra on the phone earlier."

I swallow hard. She did? What did she say? How did that even come up? And why wasn't that the first thing she said when I picked her up? But I don't get to ask any of those questions before she keeps going.

"She said that you didn't-but-did say you were going on a date tonight. And I'd already mentioned that I was painting my toenails, so she knew what I was up to tonight." She faces me now by turning her head and looking me in the eyes. "So I flat-out told her that I am going on a date tonight." Then she sucks her bottom lip into her mouth and bites it. "But I told her that I wouldn't tell her anything else about it and blamed that on her having Blake drama."

All I can do is stare at her. And try to keep my breathing even. I have no words. None at all. She misinterprets my speechlessness though.

"I'm sorry. I should have told her, but you weren't there and I wasn't ready. It came out of nowhere. But I thought you'd be happy that I almost—"

"I am," I say, interrupting her. "I am. So"—my voice cracks, so I try again—"so happy."

It's a step in the right direction. She didn't lie about me. She didn't tell the whole story, but she didn't deny anything. Which is most definitely a step in the right direction. And I'm so happy that I could cry. But I clear my throat and tighten my grip on her fingers. Then I let her hand go and reach forward to hug her. I won't dare kiss her here, though the fear that I'm about to do that flashes on her face before I wrap my one arm around her. I can hug her though, so I do. Tight. The only way I can show my love for her and her impressive forward progression right now.

"Thank you," I whisper in her ear.

She tightens her hold on me to tell me she heard me. Then she springs away from me when someone knocks on the window. When my eyes pop open, I see her dad standing outside my car.

"Everything okay?" he asks loudly to be heard through the window.

"Yeah!" she squeaks out as she opens her door, her voice too high-pitched to be considered normal. "I was just giving Patti a hug because she"—she pauses when she steps out of my car, but I think it's more of a delay tactic—"drove me here. It was nice of her to pick me up." Once she's done, she hugs her dad too.

He laughs lightly and wraps his arm around his daughter as I get out of the car. "It definitely was nice of her," he says before winking at me over the top of my car.

I smile back and then make my way around my car to them.

"I'm glad you're in a better mood today, Zoeybell. I don't like to see you so stressed out," he tells her. Then he pulls back from her.

She waves him off. "I know. Just a lot going on at work." She kisses him on his cheek and then walks past him to go inside the house.

Her dad hangs behind and throws his arm around my shoulder, squeezing me to him as we walk to the door. "Hi, Patti."

"Hey, Dad," I say back, accepting his warm, loving hug.

"Thanks for taking care of our girl."

"That's what I'm here for," I reply.

On the step before the doorway, he stops us and faces me. After a quiet moment, he rubs his hand over his mouth. "Do you know what's going on with her? She's been moody and stressed. I think it's more than work, but she doesn't want us to worry."

For the second time today, I swallow hard, struck speechless. I open my mouth to answer him, but I shut it right away so nothing "bad" comes out. I center myself and try again. "She'll have to tell you herself, though I can assure you that she's healthy and has me in her corner one hundred percent."

He releases a relieved breath and startles me by suddenly hugging me with a really tight grip. Like, I can barely breathe.

"Oh, thank the Lord," he whispers in a shaky voice. When he leans back, he keeps his arms on my shoulders. "Her mother and I are so thankful for you. You're the sister we couldn't give her and a daughter we were never blessed with. You're the best thing we could ask for for our daughter." Then he kisses me on my cheek and gestures with his head toward the inside of their house. "I'll make sure Beth makes your favorite meal next Friday."

I press my lips into a thin line as I attempt to smile and nod. But my heart is stuck in my throat. I finally understand why Zo's so scared of disappointing them. Yes, they're her parents, and yes, they seem to have their priorities backwards, but they're kind, loving, giving people otherwise. They've loved her all of her life and me for most of mine. They truly want what's best for her, even if their idea of what's best doesn't match up with her version. Or mine.

When their love is shining on me, I can't deny that need to please them too. But the day will come where they know the truth about what's really eating at their daughter. And I hope Zo and I strong enough together to withstand their disapproval. Though I already know I'll selfishly spend some time hoping they won't disapprove of me personally.

CHAPTER 10

Patti

"Honestly, I don't care which movie we see," I tell Zo for the fifth time, rolling my eyes. "You pick. Whatever you want."

"You don't have to be rude about it," she mumbles under her breath as she unbuckles her seat belt.

As she gets out of the car, I say, "I'm not being rude, Zed." Then I mumble, "I just really don't care which fucking movie you choose," to myself before opening my car door.

"You sure sound like it to me." She throws her arms in the air. "Seriously, what's been up with you tonight? You were fine earlier, but once we got to my parents' house, it was..."

I tune her out as we approach the movie theater. Yes, I've been weird. All night, I've been thinking about the very thing that worries her to her core. And I understand it now. I don't think it's enough for me to break things off with her, but I certainly see where she's coming from. This, however, doesn't feel like the time to bring it up. Not on a first date. Can't we be normal on our first date? For shit's sake.

She's still going on when I open the door for her, but as soon as I walk in, I find a familiar face in the line to buy movie tickets. Two of them, actually.

"Are you even listening to me?" Zo whines.

I grab her wrist and pull her back toward me.

"Ouch. What the heck, Patti?" She tugs out of my grip and rubs her wrist. Then she finally looks right at me.

I'm frozen in my spot, staring at the backs of Lyra's and Blake's heads. When Zo realizes I'm not moving or playing around, she follows my gaze. And gasps. But then she moves us out of the way of the doorway and takes a breath.

"We're not doing anything abnormal, remember?" she says. "Friends go to the movies all the time."

"Uh, yeah," I spit out, "but you're forgetting the part where we both told Lyra that we had dates tonight."

Her eyes flash wide for a moment. She regains her composure and says, "Okay, fine. Maybe they were shitty and we both met up here." One of her eyebrows rises, and then they both fall when she scrunches her forehead. "Hey. Wait a minute. Why am I being the logical one here?"

Under normal circumstances, I'd laugh at that. Because she has a point. I'm usually the one to think things through, not get ahead of myself. She's the worrywart. The one who overthinks things to death. But, after everything that came up with her folks earlier and now this, we've switched places. And I don't know how much more I can take tonight.

When I peek around her, Lyra and Blake are handing their tickets to the attendant. A few moments later, they're out of sight. But what if they decide they want popcorn and have to come back out here? What if Lyra gets thirsty and sends Blake for something to drink and he runs into Zo while I'm in the bathroom?

My god. Is this how Zo feels twenty-four-seven? Good grief. No wonder she has panic attacks. I might have one right now.

Zo's voice breaks through my thoughts. "Are they here on a date? Is that what she decided on when she got off the phone with us?"

"Stop!" I say too loudly, throwing my hands in the air. So I quiet my voice. "Just stop." Then I shove the door open hard enough for both of us to walk through it. "I don't know, but we could have been caught tonight. I was too distracted, and this could have—"

"Hey." Zo pulls on my arm as we go back to the car.

When I stop and face her, she slides her hand down my arm and interlaces our fingers.

"I'm not usually the one to say this," she says, a small smile on her lips, "but come back to now."

That phrase is supposed to work in a situation just like this one. I don't know if she knows where the phrase came from, but I've been using it on her for years now, and it works. And I do want to relax, tug her to me, and kiss her right on the mouth in front of everyone. Prove to her that we're stronger no matter what is thrown in our path because we're together. In my heart right now, I'm just not sure I feel that. With or without the reminder of being present with her.

For show, I inhale deeply. But the air in my lungs does give me a moment of peace to stop and think about things differently. I love Zo. That's for sure. I love her family too though. And I love our friends, but I don't think they're going to care. Not in a bad way, anyway. However, my love for Zo—does it come before my love for everyone else? Does it win above all others?

As I exhale, the answer nearly brings me to my knees.

"We should go home and talk," I tell her, squeezing her fingers. I don't smile because I'm all business right now.

"Okay," she drawls, stretching the word out for a few seconds. "But you're freaking me out now. And you know how I get when I worry."

"I know, Zed." I start to walk toward the car again. "Come on."

***

89

Zo

I don't know what the heck is going on with her, but when we almost get caught and she is the one to freak out? Something's obviously wrong. And, now, she wants to go home and talk. When we're supposed to be going on our first date. When we're supposed to be enjoying our time as a new couple. When I was finally starting to wrap my head around all of this.

Now, she wants to talk. Now of all times.

Oh god. What if she's about to break up with me? What if, after all of these years she's wanted to be with me, she finally got a taste and I'm not at all what she thought she wanted? What if I've spent the last several weeks doing things my parents would be ashamed of with a woman and she's going to leave me? What if I finally admitted to myself how I feel about her and I'm not enough?

Suddenly, when we pull into my driveway, my lungs lock up and I can't pull any air in. Not a single ounce. My chest constricts with the effort it's taking to attempt to breathe, and I close my eyes to make the world stop spinning, but the lack of oxygen is making me lightheaded. I'm vaguely aware of Patti putting her car into park and reaching for her seat belt, but I'm mainly trying to stop my heart from pounding right out of my chest. Though I don't have the first clue on how to do that if I can't control my breathing.

"Zed?" Patti asks, but her voice sounds far away, like I'm underwater and not sitting in her car. "What's going on? Are you okay?"

Frantically, I shake my head. But I'm already super dizzy and the movement makes it so much worse. Squeezing my eyes shut, I rest my head on the headrest and try to breathe, but I can't for the life of me calm down. My shallow breaths are doing nothing to make me feel like I'm getting enough oxygen, so I lean forward and put my head between my knees.

"Oh my god. What do I do?" she questions as she puts her hand on my back. "Zo? What am I supposed to do?"

"Turn the air on," I tell her, though my words are muffled because my head's in my lap. But I need the cool air. I'm sweating everywhere, the scorching heat inside me becoming unbearable.

What the hell is going on with me?

"Okay," she says, jumping into action.

The air conditioner kicks on a second later and cools my heated skin. But there's still one problem cooler air won't fix. I can't freaking breathe. My tongue is also starting to tingle for some reason. And I'm this close to blacking out.

"ER," I croak out.

"What?" she asks. "I'm sorry. I can't hear you."

I sit up a little, as much as my dizzy head will allow. The movement makes the world spin the other way, and that causes my stomach to lurch. I take some more shallow breaths just to keep breathing, but I'm fairly certain I'm about to die again. Like, really certain. So I need to go to the hospital. Right now.

"ER," I repeat just above my legs. "Take me to the ER."

She's frozen for a moment, but then she puts her seat belt back on and backs out of my driveway. Her right hand rubs my back while she drives, and that's my only anchor to this world. The only thing keeping me rooted here, conscious and hoping to live through this terrifying episode. Because, if I'm not going to die right now, I need something to live for. And it just might be the hand on my back.

So I plead with whoever will listen. *Don't let her break up with me. I'll be better. I'll be different—whoever she needs me to be. I'll tell whoever she wants me to tell. I'll do anything for this woman. I haven't had enough time with her, and I haven't told her I love her yet. So don't take me away now. I need more time.*

I chant these things over and over again until it's my

turn to be seen by the ER doctor. What a great first date.

***

Patti

"Well, the good news is that no one's ever died from a panic attack," the ER doctor tells my girlfriend.

"If it's going to happen for a first time, it'll be to me," she replies, not a drop of humor in her tone.

His smile is comforting—to me, at least. "Let's get you set up with an antianxiety medication that'll help keep you calm. Just a low dose for now to see how it works for you, okay?" He puts a hand on her shoulder. "You're going to be fine."

She might be fine in the future, but we need her to be fine right now. Which leads me to some questions.

"Are there things we can do in the meantime while the medication kicks in?" I peek at her from my spot in the extra chair in the room, but she's still staring at her legs. "Stress management, breathing exercises? What about discovering her triggers?"

She finally looks at me, and her expression says *How would you know about those things?*

"What?" I shrug. "I started Googling stuff while we were waiting to be seen."

I swear I see the hint of a smile curl the corners of her lips, but then the doctor answers my questions.

"Yes, actually." he says. "Those are great things to do right now. Meditation, keeping stress low, practicing some yoga. Try those things as well. And there are several breathing techniques that can help stop panic attacks in their tracks." He turns back to Zo, smiling warmly at her. "You have a pretty good friend in this one." He points his manila folder with her chart at me. "I think you're going to be okay."

"Hear that, Zed? You're gonna live." I wink at her, but suddenly, she's all ice again.

The doctor backs up toward the door. "If there's nothing else, I'll go get that prescription for you. Then you can get home, rest, and relax. Okay?"

She nods once. Sharply. And continues staring at her lap, wringing her hands on top of her thighs. Once the doctor has shut the door, she rounds on me.

"I really thought I was going to die, Patti. If you haven't had a panic attack, then you have no idea what this feels like. And it literally feels like you're going to drop dead."

I throw my hands up in surrender. "Whoa. Okay. Sorry."

"Sorry for what?" she spits back at me. "Sorry for wasting your time here at the ER all night? Sorry for finally getting what you wanted only to realize it's nothing like what you thought it would be? Or are you sorry for the words you're going to use when you dump me?"

With wide eyes, I stare back at the crazy person who's taken my girlfriend's body over. Granted, she just had some weird death-defying experience. But shit. What in the ever-loving hell is she talking about? Dump her? Not what I thought it would be?

"Um, what?" is all I manage to say in answer.

"Don't give me that," she says, her words tight as she fidgets with her fingers. "Everyone knows what 'we have to talk' means." Then she scoffs. "And to think I was falling in love with you."

Every smartass retort I have dies on my tongue when the L-word comes into play. Those dead words dry my mouth out. I'm speechless, which is good because I couldn't possibly speak right now even if I tried.

"Thanks for at least sparing me that much. I might be able to recover from this once you drop me off at home." She shakes her head. "Never mind. Better yet, I'll just Uber it home inst—"

"Okay, enough!" I say loudly enough to cut her stream of nonsense off.

The doctor chooses now to knock on the door and come back into the room, so my potential tirade is cut short. We'll finish this in the car, and that's exactly the look I give her right before the doctor focuses on us.

"All right. Here's your prescription," he says, handing her a sheet of paper. Then he hands her another. "And here's a good breathing technique you can try when you feel another panic attack coming on. You know the signs now, so practice your breathing and you'll be fine. Come back and see us if anything else happens, okay?" There's his warm, friendly smile again. "No stress. Doctor's orders." He points a teasing finger at her as his smile grows. Then he winks.

"Thanks," Zo tells him, clutching the two pieces of paper in her hands.

As the doctor backs away to the door, she hops off the hospital bed. While she's picking her purse up off the counter, I get a peek at her toenails and remember that this was supposed to be a date. We were supposed to see a movie, hold hands in the dark, and maybe sneak a kiss like we were teenagers trying not to get caught by our parents. This was supposed to be a fun night for us, and instead, it went to shit. Ended up with a trip to the hospital and everything.

Will this be a story we'll tell our friends' grandchildren? Our own if we adopt? Will we even be together through the night? One look at Zo's face leaves me with no clue. But she used the L-word, and maybe it's playing dirty, but I'm putting that in my pocket for future use if I have to.

Once we're back out to my car, I hit the unlock button on my fob, but I grab her door handle so she can't get in just yet. "You're an expensive date," I say, trying to joke with her. It might be the wrong time, but I haven't been known for my timing lately.

Somehow, though, it penetrates her tough-chick exterior and she lets out a small giggle. Which turns into a chuckle that morphs into a full-belly laugh. There's the girl I've wanted to see all night. No, I haven't been a bundle of joy, but she, per the doctor's orders, doesn't need more stress in her life. She needs to laugh more, feel freer and more joy. She doesn't need a tough conversation that'll freak her out. She doesn't need my worry to be piled on top of her own.

So I open her car door, let her get in, and then take us back to her place. No drama in sight.

CHAPTER 11

Zo

"Oh my. That feels…" My words trail off as I try to think of one that accurately describes how delicious this bath water is on my skin. Instead, I leave it at that, resting my head back on the rolled-up towel behind my neck, and smile.

As soon as we got back from the ER, Patti took me straight to my bathroom, where she drew a hot bath and lit candles to keep the lighting dim. No stress, the doctor said. And it seems she's taking him seriously.

I'll take it seriously too. I don't know how yet, considering that everything about my relationship is drama right now. And, even after we tell people, it still might be stressful drama. But, like Patti reminded me in the car, I need to stay focused on what I can control. Right now, I can control how relaxed I am in this tub of gloriously warm water.

Perhaps I'm ignoring the fact that I told her I was falling in love with her. And I might also be ignoring the fact that I accused her of wanting to break up with me. I don't know if she's here because the doctor said I don't need any stress and she doesn't want to stress me out. But I don't want to know yet. I just want to enjoy one more night where Patti and I are together. No drama. No stress. Just us.

I peek over at her. She's sitting on the toilet seat lid, flicking through websites Google spit out after her search of stress management skills. Taking a bath was on the list, but she's finding other things I can work on so I don't panic anymore. The promise of not panicking anymore sounds far too good to be true, but I'll do just about anything to keep the attacks at bay. I'd go so far as to say telling my parents I'm now a lesbian would be less scary than having another panic attack.

Am I a lesbian? Am I bisexual? Oh god. I don't even know. Wait. Deep breath. I'm supposed to be relaxing. Not stressing. None of that matters right now, in this moment. I can't worry about the future and what might happen, Patti says. I can only think about what's happening right now. Which is why she always says that phrase to me. Which reminds me.

"Hey," I quietly say to get her attention.

Absentmindedly, she says, "Yeah?" She's still engrossed in whatever website she's found about treating panic attacks. At least, I assume she's still doing that.

"Wanna join me? I want to ask you something."

By join, I mean the conversation. But she slips her shoes off, sets her phone on the counter with the screen still on, and starts to unzip her dress. That's fine by me though. That kind of join works too.

Once her dress has fallen to the floor, she works her panties down, her gaze still glued to the phone. She swipes the screen to keep reading and then unhooks her bra. Completely naked, she finishes reading something on her phone before walking toward the tub. When she has a hand on the towel under my head, I sit forward so she can slip in behind me. The water level rises as she gets in, and the bubbles nearly touch my chin.

Wrapping her arms around me, she says, "I was just reading about the AWARE technique of overcoming panic attacks. It's about—"

"Wait," I say, laughing lightly. I appreciate her concern, but I want to focus on something good right now. "I said I want to ask you about something."

"Oh, sorry." She readjusts behind me. "What's up?"

I run my fingers along her arms under the water. "I don't know where your phrase came from. Why have you always said that to me?"

"Come back to now?" she asks, setting her chin on my shoulder. Her breath tickles my ear.

I tilt my head to the left and nod.

Her throat bobs as she swallows against my shoulder. Then she tilts her head the opposite way of mine and takes a deep breath. "My grandma used to say that to me. After my parents died, I'd wait by the door for them to come back. I was young, so I didn't quite understand what death meant, so my grandma explained it as they're no longer in my 'now.' They might be in my 'later,' but they weren't here now, like she and my grandpa were. So she'd remind me to come back to now and be with her instead of waiting for my parents because they weren't coming back."

So much for relaxing. A tear slips down my right cheek, which she notices. She puts her lips on my cheek to catch the tear and kisses me.

"That's such a sweet story," I say. Then an oddly timed laugh bubbles up from my throat. "Ridiculously sad, but sweet."

She laughs too, squeezing me tight. "I know, right? And you're not supposed to be stressing out."

I can't help but smile at that. Then I face her and, in a soft, gentle tone, say, "Thank you."

"For what?" she questions.

"Everything," I say. "For running this bath. For lighting the candles. For Googling how to fix me. For being so attentive. For salvaging our first date. For not breaking up with me. For reminding me to—"

"What?" she asks, her eyebrows scrunched low on her

forehead.

I look away from her. "Well, you didn't let me finish."

"Why are you thanking me for not breaking up with you?" She brings her hand out of the water to turn my face back to hers. "You said something similar at the hospital and I thought it was ridiculous then too."

I open my mouth, but I close it when nothing comes out. Then I try again and finally say, "You said we needed to talk," in a small voice. I swallow over a lump in my throat and wipe another tear from my eye. "What else could that mean?"

"Oh, Zed," she sighs. "I promise you—the talk wasn't about that. You are my woman through and through." Squeezing me to her, she rubs my nose with hers and then kisses my lips. "Anything I was going to say earlier can wait until we get your stress level under control."

I'm not sure if I'm relieved that we're not breaking up or more stressed because she won't tell me what's going on with her. She's right though. If it can wait right now, it should. I'm exhausted, and this bath is doing the relaxation trick. Especially with Patti's warm body wrapped around me. So I nod. We'll talk about it later.

"Hey," Patti says, her eyes flashing wide and a smile curling her lips. "You know what else I read was good for relaxation?" She raises her eyebrows as she trails her fingers down my middle. All the way down until they reach my core.

I release a deep sigh, appreciating the way she's thinking. Especially when one finger lands right on my clit. She knows exactly how and where to touch me, exactly how to please me. In the last several weeks, she's become something of an expert. And I allow her expertise to relax me all the way to a shuddering, mind-blowing climax.

Then, when my eyes won't stay open any longer, she helps me out of the tub, into a towel, and under the covers, where I fall right asleep in her arms—my favorite place in this whole world.

***

Patti

"How was your honeymoon?" Zo asks as she hugs Shiree the following Thursday at the bar. "I want to hear all about it!"

I share her enthusiasm, but it's mostly because neither of us wants to talk about us. And Lyra, who's sick tonight, isn't here to distract Shiree with questions, so it's fallen upon us to pick up the slack. And we can't talk about Lyra, either. She hasn't told Shiree about Blake yet, so that's yet another secret we have to keep. Luckily, Zo seems happy to take the job of keeping Shiree distracted. Or she's just more desperate than I am to keep the conversation away from our relationship right now.

"It was so much fun! Fiji is gorgeous beyond words, you guys," Shiree gushes. "And the alone time was..." She winks at us. It's exaggerated, and I'm both happy for her and nauseated at the same time.

Zo cracks up though. It's pretty fake, but I'm probably the only one who can tell.

"Tell me more!" she squeals. "I want to hear alllll about it!"

Shiree launches into a few tales about their travels, and I nurse my beer, leaning my elbows on our table. When it's gone, I lift it up and signal that I'm going to get another. I can't concentrate on what she's saying anyway, so it's best if I don't have to pretend. Especially because I'm already pretending about so many other things.

When I get to the bar, I order another beer and wait for the bartender to get it. Once he returns with my bottle, I go to give him my debit card, but someone next to me shouts, "Put that one on my tab!" over the music.

I turn toward the voice and find Kimber two people down. She smiles at me, and I politely smile back before declining her offer.

"That's okay." I shake my head. "I got it."

"I insist," she says.

I weigh the pros and cons, but what are the cons of accepting a free drink from someone who knows I'm seeing someone already? Maybe it's my foul mood, but I can't think of a single one right now. So I give in and shrug.

Her smile gets wider as the bartender disappears to add my beer to her bill. While I'm pocketing my card, she steps around the two people between us and squeezes her body and her drink next to me and mine. It's a tight fit, so I twist until I'm sideways to keep some space between us. That doesn't stop her from hugging me though.

"Hey!" she shouts near my ear. "It's good to see you drinking something other than coffee." When she leans back, she's still smiling.

I lean closer to her. "I don't know if beer is a better option though!" I yell around a laugh. Then I pull back. "Thanks though."

She grins again and props her elbow on the bar. "So, what are you up to tonight?"

"My friend just got back from her honeymoon, so she's telling us all about it." I hook a thumb in Shiree and Zo's direction.

But Kimber's shaking her head. "No, that's not what I meant." She leans in again, putting a hand on my shoulder for some leverage. "I meant," she says right next to my ear, "what are you up to tonight?"

Oooh. I catch her drift now. And I immediately shake my head, slanting backwards so she can see me. "I'm still seeing someone," I explain. "And I plan on keeping it that way with her. For, like, ever."

Her mouth falls open, but yet again, she's smiling. "Really?" she practically squeals.

I nod, taking a swallow of my beer.

She launches toward me for another hug. Then she follows my lead, sipping her drink. "I'm so happy for you!"

An involuntary smile splits my lips and spreads all over my face. I'm sure I look like a goofball, but that's what Zo does to me. And I don't even care.

"Aww, Patti. You so deserve that," she gushes. Then her eyes go wide and she freezes. "Is she The One?"

Maybe it makes me sound lonely and pathetic that my barista knows more about my personal life than my best friends do. But it is what it is. I've told her about Zo and how much I love her, though I've never mentioned her name. And she has no idea that The One is the one who was at the coffee shop that morning we were there together. Which would probably make Zo happy. So much of me wants to point her out in the crowd though.

I won't. But my gaze must slide in her direction anyway, because the next thing I know, Kimber's looking her way. Then she swings her wide-eyed gaze back to me.

"Hey, she looks famil—oh!" Her mouth forms a perfectly round O, and she points in Zo's direction. "The one from The Steam Room that day? She's The One? She knows now?" she asks, referencing our previous run-in at the coffee shop.

I swat her hand down. "She's not ready yet is all." After a breath, I say, "There are some...complications."

Kimber's mouth forms a smaller O now. "Are you sure that's it?"

"One hundred percent positive," I tell her, no hesitation at all in my tense response.

She puts her hands up in front of chest. "Okay. Just looking out for you."

I lower some of my defenses and relax my shoulders. And probably my facial expression. "Thanks. It's going to be okay. I just have to be patient, and she's worth it."

As she takes a sip of her drink, I bring my bottle to my

lips. And we both kind of smile at each other. Things are good, and they'll only get better. Maybe I don't know when yet, but they will. Except, when I look over at my friends, Zo's shooting daggers at me with her eyes and Shiree has no clue as she yammers on.

"Look," I say, reluctantly sliding my gaze back to Kimber. "I should probably get back to her and my friends. But I don't have to make you promise not to—"

She mimes zipping her grinning lips and throwing a key away. So I don't bother finishing my sentence. Instead, I give her a kind, relieved smile, say thanks once more for the beer by tipping it in her direction, and nod before heading back to our table. When I get there, Shiree's in the middle of yet another honeymoon story, which I can't say I'm sorry I missed. I love my friend, but my mind is certainly elsewhere.

She stops midsentence and looks at me. "You were gone a long time, lady. I thought you were bringing everyone drinks." She's smiling, so I don't think she's upset—just making an observation.

One Zo obviously made too, if her cool expression is anything to go by.

"No worries," Shiree says, waving it off. "I'll go get some. A Sea Breeze for me. Zo, you want another?"

She nods vigorously as I take a sip of my beer, and I nearly choke on it. Shiree doesn't seem to notice before she goes to the bar for more drinks. Which leaves me alone with my girlfriend no one knows about. Except for Kimber. But I trust her, so I'm not worried about that.

I don't have time to wonder if I'm relieved that someone knows or nervous that someone else might have overheard something that'd make them put two and two together though. Zo leans across the table, folding her arms on top of it, and flicks her gaze over at Kimber.

"Have a nice chat?" she asks, raising her eyebrows at me. Her tone is only slightly accusatory.

I bring my bottle to my lips, take a swig, and nod. "She

thought it was funny to see me drinking something other than coffee."

Her eyebrows go up even higher on her forehead. "That's it?"

Shrugging, I say, "Yeah. What did you think it was?"

She holds my stare for a few nearly uncomfortable moments before she shrugs. "Like Shiree pointed out, you were gone a while. And you looked pretty friendly."

"She's a friendly person, Zed." I put my beer on the table a little too hard, and it clanks when it hits the wood. "Do you not trust me?"

She releases a deep breath and sits back in her chair, her hands staying on the table, palms down. With her gaze on me, she says, "Of course I do." Then she mumbles something like, "It's her I don't trust."

I'm not one hundred percent sure that's what she said, so I leave it alone. I don't need her to trust anyone else as long as she trusts me. This whole thing is new to her, and she's never been this serious—especially this fast—with someone before. So I get it, but I won't entertain it.

"All that matters is that I love you," I say loud enough so only she can hear me, covering on of her hand with mine.

She jerks away from my touch and then downs the last drops of her drink in preparation for the next one, avoiding my gaze. My immediate reaction is to feel hurt that she'd reject me like that. But, after a tense, painful moment, I remember where we are. Who we're with. What we're doing here. I remember that we have to hide who we are. What we feel. How much we care.

I remember again how much is at stake. What we have to lose. What—rather, who—we might destroy with our secret.

One of us has to drive, so I decide to stop for the night. Plus, drinking when I'm in a shitty mood only puts me in a shittier mood. So I slide my bottle to the side. Then I lean closer to her, ready to admit the rest of what happened.

That I told someone about us and she was happy for us. That the whole world won't end or come crashing down on her just because we're together. But I think better of it. This isn't the time or the place, and Shiree's probably—

"Now, we're topped off," she says cheerily as she joins us again. She slides Zo's drink to her, which she accepts but doesn't drink any of it right away.

Instead, she gazes down at the floor, clearly all in her head about something. I want to tell her that alcohol is definitely on the "don't" list when anxiety and panic attacks are the norm. As far as I know, she hasn't started the medication. Thank goodness. But she's a grown woman. She can make her choices. And, like an obedient dog, I'll be there to see her through them.

Shiree looks between us both. "What's going on here?"

"Nothing," Zo and I say at the same time.

Zo was doing great at deflecting earlier, but I guess it's my turn.

"I think Lyra's finally seeing someone," I tell Shiree, knowing that'll move this in a new direction. And I'm not wrong.

Shiree that's that bit of info and runs with it, seemingly pleased that her "just sex" advice must have finally helped her move on from Roger. Which works as far as averting her from the truth of the matter goes. However, I'm just not sure how long that's going to last.

I'm not sure how long any of it is going to last.

CHAPTER 12

Zo

It's amazing what sleep can do for your perspective on things. And for a hangover, but that's beside the point. I've been getting enough sleep lately because Patti and I haven't been having sleepovers every night. Our sleepovers weren't all that full of sleep. Now, I can actually go to bed at a decent hour.

However, I don't sleep as well as I do when we're together. I sleep, but it's fitful. I wake up and forget she's not here, so I end up staying awake for a while. Then I fall back into a dreamless, restless sleep.

So I'm sleeping, but it's not great. And that's not great for my anxiety and panic attacks. Luckily, I haven't had one of those since the last one that put me in the ER a month and a half ago, but that doesn't mean another one isn't on the horizon. It's just been easier to manage now that Patti and I have cooled things off a bit. Not officially in any capacity. It's how things seem to have shaken out right now. She has a big project at work due soon, so she's used our time apart for that. And I've used it for not having panic attacks. And that's about it.

She's skipped a couple of Thirsty Thursdays, and she's even missed a few Friday dinners. But she wasn't always consistent with being at dinner in the first place, so my parents haven't thought much of it. Especially because she told them how busy she is at work right now. I'm worried that she's using it more as an excuse though. So I finally cave in and go over to her place after another Friday dinner without her.

When I bang on her door, I hear her footsteps start to head in my direction. She must take a second to look through the peephole, because the doorknob turns slightly, there's a momentary pause, and then it turns again. As soon as the door is open enough for me to see her, I'm nearly brought to tears.

"What happened?" I ask, a sob escaping my lips. I've turned into a blubbering mess in a matter of seconds.

That's all it takes for Patti to put her arms around me and bring me inside. She ushers me over to the couch, and we both sit. She keeps her arms in a tight circle around my shoulders, and I sob into her neck, letting the emotion of the past six weeks finally hit me. A deep inhale gives me the fix of her lemon scent I've been craving. And a soothing, relaxing feeling washes over me in her embrace.

This is exactly what I've needed, what I've missed, this entire time.

She places her lips on my temple and then rests her chin on the top of my head. "Did you have another panic attack?" she asks, going straight to the point.

I shake my head, my tears spreading on the collar of her shirt.

"Then what's going on?"

All I can do is shrug.

She doesn't like that answer, apparently, because she pulls away from me and holds me by my shoulders. "Zo, what's going on?" she repeats, using my real name.

Which snaps me out of it. I yank my sleeves down so I can wipe my eyes with them. When they're dry enough, I scoot back on the couch and pinch the bridge of my nose.

"I just don't understand," I tell her and then drop my

hand to my lap. "How have we barely spoken in the last several weeks? Why are you avoiding me?"

She huffs out a deep, long breath through her nose. "I'm not avoiding you—"

"That's bullshit and you know it," I spit out at her.

"Take it down a notch, will you?" She crosses her arms over her chest. "You're not coming into my house and making a scene right now."

"Then what am I supposed to do? You haven't called, texted, or come by. You're missing events you'd normally attend. What do you want me to do?"

She throws her arms out to her sides, sitting closer to the edge so as not to hit the couch. "I want you to stop living in fear!" she shouts. "And I want to stop living there too!"

I gulp and bring my hand to my chest as if I've been physically wounded. Because it certainly feels like I have. My heart aches; this was my fault. Just like I suspected. But the conformation hurts deep down to my bones.

But wait. "Why are you living there too?" I ask her. "What are you afraid of?"

Her sigh is long and deep. Then she crumples against the back of the couch, totally defeated. "Everything you're afraid of," she simply says, her eyes closed.

My breath catches in my throat. "What? Since when?"

"Since the Friday dinner the night I took you to the emergency room," she admits. Then she opens her eyes. "I had a talk with your dad that scared me straight."

My eyes go wide as hers fly open. When her gaze meets mine, I almost burst out laughing.

"Not literally, mind you." She gives me a small smirk.

I can't help but give her one back. The mood has officially been lightened, and I couldn't be more thankful.

"Okay..." I say, stretching the word out to gather my thoughts. "So, why didn't you talk to me? Why was avoiding me the better option?"

"Like I said," she tells me, her palms on her thighs as she sits up, "I wasn't avoiding you. It was just easier if we didn't see each other as much."

"Sounds an awful lot like avoiding me," I mumble, but it's in a teasing tone.

She rolls her eyes, her lips slightly turned up. "Tomato, tomahto." She laughs lightly before going back to all business. "Seriously, Zed. Your panic attacks and anxiety were bad. You had to be rushed to the fucking emergency room over this shit. So, to me, it was easier to not have that talk and just let things…simmer."

"Well, they're boiling now." I reach out to cover one of her hands with one of mine.

When our fingers touch, I'm reminded of exactly why I came here tonight. This small, simple touch tells me everything I need to know about why we're supposed to be together. We're electric. We're on fire. We're so right no matter who thinks we're wrong. No matter who I can't bring myself to tell about us.

She links our fingers together. "I'm sorry. I got scared. That's all."

"Scared of what?" I ask, squeezing her hand. "And why is it okay for you to run away when you're scared but I have to face it?"

"I know," she huffs out on a deep exhale, slumping forward. "I'm a hypocrite. But I didn't know what else to do. And I didn't have my best friend to talk it over with."

"You always have me," I softly remind her.

"That's not what I meant." Her torso twists so she's facing me, and she readjusts our hands so she has a better grip. "You haven't been yourself lately. You've been anxious, sad, even jealous. Those aren't normal Zed traits. And I'm not saying I don't like them. I've loved you through a lot worse. But…" She hesitates, takes a breath. "But you have to be comfortable with who you are and who we are together before I can risk telling your parents with you."

When her words hit me, I gasp and my free hand flies to my mouth. She's totally right. In the middle of all of this, even though I knew it, I didn't realize that she'd be just as scared to lose my parents too. Of course I know how much they mean to her, but like an idiot, I didn't put it together that she'd end up with no one if things don't go well with my parents and we don't work out.

"Oh my," I breathe out around my fingers. "I've been such an idiot."

"You haven't," she reassures me. "This whole thing has been difficult to navigate, but I won't do it until you're completely in. You've had one foot in, but you have to—"

"Jump." I drop my hand so she'll understand me this time. "Jump. I'll jump in. I'm ready."

She's already shaking her head though. "You've said similar things before, Zed. Forgive me if I'm not ready to believe you."

Again, she's right. Absolutely right. No matter how hard I wish she weren't, I can't change it. It's in the past. But I can make the future different. And we can start right now.

"So let's do this." I straighten my spine. "We'll make up, because I've heard make-up sex is pretty good."

That cracks a smile on her lips. Which teases my own out too. Then I take a deep breath and prepare to drop this bomb.

"And then we can call an emergency Thirsty Thursday group meeting for tonight and tell Shiree and Lyra about us."

The moment the words are all out of my mouth, we both react. My heart starts pounding a mile a minute, and sweat makes my underarms tingle. But her reaction is the clear winner. That crack of a smile threatens to turn into a full-blown, beaming, mile-wide grin. She holds it back, but it's obvious she has to force it away.

"You're sure?" she questions, keeping her features

neutral. And rightfully so.

I nod vigorously, ignoring the panic building in me. "I want to prove to you that I mean it."

She runs her free hand through her hair, taking a moment to process this. Then she shrugs while staring at the floor. "I mean, okay." She faces me, the hint of a smile on her lips. "If you're sure."

"I am." I scoot closer to her, tightening my hold on her hand.

And, this time, the only response I get is her lips on mine for the first time in far, far too long.

***

Patti

"Oh my god!" she shouts just before my name leaves her lips. "You have to stop. You're gonna kill me." She's panting, out of breath, but completely satisfied.

I kiss her inner thigh. Then her hipbone. Then near her belly button. My tongue comes out and traces a path up her torso and over the swell of one breast as I crawl my way up to her. I switch directions, circle one nipple, and then suck on the other, all the while keeping my gaze on hers.

She's in a happy, euphoric daze. Her eyelids are heavy, and they droop closed. Her red hair is fanned out over my pillow, right where it belongs. A gentle, soft smile curves her full lips, and I grin too because I put it there. So I kiss those lips just because I can.

"Goodness gracious, woman," she says, a slight gravelly tone to her voice. Her lips brush mine as she speaks. "I lost count after four, but my downstairs can't handle any more."

I plant kisses down her neck. "Good." Kiss. "That's the idea." Another kiss. This one on her collarbone.

She lazily wraps her arms around my neck, which prevents me from going any farther down her body. "Is it

111

ever your turn?"

I whip my head up to look her in her eyes. "Woman. Eating your pussy is my turn. God, I love it."

Her giggle warms me from the inside out. I love it so much when she's real with me. When she lets her guard down and doesn't worry about everything so damn much. That's when she's my favorite Zo. When she's my Zed.

"Seriously though. What time is it?" she asks. "It's gonna be too late to call Shiree and Lyra soon."

"I don't know." I bring my knees up so I can kneel in a straddle around her hips. Then I reach over to my nightstand and grab my phone. "Holy hell. It's after one already. Officially Saturday."

Her eyes widen as she grips my waist. "Geez!" she exclaims, sliding her hands up my body to my boobs. She squeezes and massages them, and my eyes drift closed at the pleasure of her hands on me.

"We're never going to leave this bed if you keep doing that," I practically moan.

She counters with, "We're never going to leave this weird funk if we don't at least try to call them."

"Is that really a bad thing? Staying here, naked and warm? Hmm?" I finally peek at her with one eye.

One eyebrow is up, and she's looking at me like *Seriously?*

"Okay, okay," I say, getting ready to pull Shiree's number up.

Then the weirdest thing happens. My phone starts ringing in my hand. We both jump, and I almost drop my phone on the bed. Luckily, I keep my hold of it. When I see who it is, my eyes go wide and I gasp.

"It's Shiree!" I whisper-yell at Zo like Shiree can hear me even though I haven't answered the phone.

"Oh my goodness! It's like a sign or something!" Zo quietly shrieks.

When I just stare at Zo with my wide-eyed stare, she

wiggles around to get me to snap out of it.

"Answer the phone!" she whisper-shouts, giving me a *duh* look.

Snap out of it, I do. And then I push the button to answer the phone. "Hello?" I hope I sounded normal.

"Hey," Shiree says, not sounding like herself. "I'm glad you're awake. Can you come to my house, like, now? It's kind of an emergency in a Lyra-and-I-desperately-need-our-friends kind of way."

I raise my eyebrows and stare at a spot on the wall. "Yeah, sure. I'll call Zo, and if she's up, we'll be there shortly."

"Okay, great. Thanks."

"Is everything okay?" I ask.

"Well…" She hesitates a little too long, but I wait it out. "I just found out I'm pregnant, actually."

"Oh wow. That's…awesome." It came out awkwardly, but I was caught off guard, so…

"Yeah, thanks. We'll see you when you get here, okay?" Then she hangs up before I can reply.

I drop my phone into my other hand and gaze at it without actually noticing it. Because this is yet another time where Zo and I can't come clean about our relationship. Not when it sounds like our friends are going through a hard time. Not when they need us for emotional support.

Except that we need them too. Holding Zo up by myself was getting difficult, though I'll do it if I have to. Now that I've left my pity party for one behind. Now that Zo's feeling more confident about being open about us. There's still a risk, but we have to start somewhere, and I thought tonight was the night. Apparently not.

"So?" Zo asks, breaking me from my thoughts. "We're going over there?"

"Yeah," I say absentmindedly. Then I shake my head to snap back into this conversation. "But it sounds like *they* need *us* right now."

"Oh." She scoots up the bed and out from under me. Leaning back on the headboard, she wraps her arms around her bent legs. "So we shouldn't tell them? Is that what you're saying?" she asks, her chin on her knees.

I shrug. "We'll feel it out when we get there, I guess. But we should get dressed now."

"Okay." Slowly, she gets up from the bed.

It might be an asshole thing to think, but I hope it's disappointment from not being able to tell our secret that's causing her reluctance. Though I'm sure there's some relief mixed in there too. And I'm sure because, even though I shouldn't, I feel both too.

~~~

Wow. They're *both* pregnant. That's...a shock. Though not really in Shiree's case. Zo and I both knew that Lyra had been seeing Blake, but we had no idea that her bouts with a stomach bug would turn out to be a baby. Holy shit.

The even bigger shock is when Blake bursts through the front door. Holy shit again. He has this blazing look in his eyes, like he's a man possessed. Possessed by his woman. He's come here to stake his claim, but he's hurt too. There's no doubt about that. But the whole scene is super uncomfortable to witness, so Zo and I stare and pick at our suddenly fascinating nails while it plays out.

Once Blake and Lyra have left, Chaz starts to make small talk.

"How are you two? I haven't seen you in a while, though Shiree's updated me on anything major."

"Has she now?" I say, knowing full well she doesn't know the half of it.

Zo clears her throat to cover for me though. "Everything's fine. It's been a long day for me, but everything's fine."

"Good, good," he says. "It's been a crazy evening here too, so if you'll excuse me, I think I'm going to head to bed." He kisses his wife on her temple and squeezes her around her shoulders. "It was great to see you two. Get home safe."

"Thanks," Zo replies.

I just lift my hand in a half-assed wave. I shouldn't be irritated with them, or with anyone else here, but it must be nice to be so open with love and uncaring of who sees you do it. They get to storm through doors for their women and kiss them openly. I, on the other hand, can't even hold Zo's hand right now or look at her in an I-like-her-as-more-than-a-friend way. Otherwise, word might spread and we might disappoint the people we love the most. God forbid...

"Ready to go?" I ask Zo, slapping a hand on her thigh. I expect her to squirm out of it, but to my surprise, she doesn't.

Instead, she covers my hand with hers. And my heart nearly leaps out of my chest.

"Yep." She turns her attention to Shiree. "As long as you're okay?"

"Oh, I'm fine." She dismisses us with a wave. "I should go to bed too. Thank you so much for coming," she tells us as we rise from the couch. She gives us both a hug and then sees us to the door.

"See you Thursday," Zo says as we step outside.

As I head toward the car and throw a wave over my shoulder, she takes my hand in hers, linking our fingers while Shiree says, "Bye!" through her open front door. While Shiree can see. It takes everything I have in me not to freeze from shock. Somehow, by a miracle, the only reaction I have is to look at Zo while we continue to walk to the car.

She's staring at the ground, but she's smiling. No, smirking. It's a sexy smirk designed to let me know how free she feels in this moment. And I now understand why men get those urges to beat on their chests when they're feeling proud of themselves.

My frustration over not telling them tonight melts away even though Shiree likely thinks nothing of it. Because my woman's holding my hand for the world to see, an action she took all on her own. And that's a great place for us to start.

CHAPTER 13

Zo

Thirsty Thursday has turned into dinner now that half of our group is pregnant. The restaurant we meet at is right next door to the bar we used to go to, so the distance is the same. But the dinner hour is much earlier than the bar hour, so I have to drive straight from work to make it on time. Usually, Patti will text me when she's on her way, because she does the same thing. Today, however, I haven't heard from her since four.

It's six fifteen when I open the restaurant doors. I'm fifteen minutes late, but Patti must be even more late. I didn't see her car in the parking lot, but it's not like I looked *that* hard. I could have missed it, though I did notice Lyra's and Shiree's cars.

Because we've been coming in every Thursday for the past two months, we've started being sat at the same table. So I make my way to our usual spot. Shiree and Lyra already have an appetizer and drinks, though I'm not surprised. It's not even that I'm late—they're eating for two. When I sit down on the empty side of the booth, Lyra points a chip at me.

"There you are," she says. "Where's Patti?" She dunks a chip in the bowl of guacamole in the middle of the table.

I shrug, setting my purse next to me on the booth seat. "I don't know." I reach into my purse and retrieve my phone, but I have no missed calls or messages from her. So I shrug again. "I still haven't heard from her, but I'm sure she'll be here."

"Good," Shiree responds, scooping some guacamole onto her chip too. "I know it's only been a week, but I love you guys." She rests a hand on her growing belly. "And I don't know how many more of these Lyra and I are going to get, so we need to promise to always be here, okay?" Unshed tears pool in her eyes.

Lyra puts her hand on Shiree's shoulder, her eyes shining too. "Don't start crying. I'll start crying if you cry, and there's nothing to cry about."

"Oh, there might be," Patti says as she plops down next to me in a huff. She folds her arms on the table and lets her head fall onto them.

"What happened?" the other two ask at the same time.

What do I do? I secretly try to comfort my secret girlfriend by resting my hand on her thigh and squeezing it.

The waiter comes by to take our order, but Shiree and Lyra shoo him away, take a couple of chips to munch on, and wait for Patti to answer them. When she finally raises her head, her mascara is smeared in the corners of her eyes and tear tracks stain her cheeks. My heart stutters and then stops, broken in two for my love.

"I got fired," she admits. Then her head falls back down onto her arms.

Relieved that it's not something more serious, I release my tense grip on her leg. And my heart resumes its normally scheduled beating. I even feel comfortable seeming more intimate with her now that the girls know that something's wrong, so I put my hand on her back and rub it in circles.

"It'll be okay, Patti. You'll find another job," I tell her, resting my head on her shoulder.

"Yeah, I'm sure you will," Shiree agrees. "You could

probably come work for NatEx. We're always hiring package handlers and drivers."

Patti lifts her head. "Do I *look* like a 'package handler'?"

The double entendre in the question almost makes me lose it, and I have to hide my face so the girls don't see my reaction. *Don't laugh. They don't mean* that *kind of package...*

"I don't know," Lyra says. "Do *I* look like a package handler?"

"I don't know what one looks like," Shiree says. "Have you ever handled packages before? When was the last time you've handled a package?"

Okay, that's it. I can't hold it back any longer. I burst into giggles against Patti's shoulder, and if I'm not mistaken, her body starts shaking with laughter. I briefly wonder if it's because she's crying, but that's laid to rest the second I look at her. Her lips are stretched into a smile, and she glances at me with a knowing gleam in her eye. The girls are laughing now too, doubled over in a giggling fit.

"Oh my god!" Lyra says between gasping breaths. "We're two kinds of package handlers, Shiree!"

Shiree cackles louder than before. "Don't make me laugh so hard! I'm gonna pee my pants!"

I might do the same, and I don't have the pregnant excuse. But, to me, Patti's clearly not any kind of package handler, so it's even funnier. But I let the laughter die down without saying anything. Shiree and Lyra know that Patti's been with women before, yet they have no idea about me. And this isn't the time or the place to say it. I'm not at all prepared, and the thoughts sober me as the other girls calm down too.

Lyra speaks up first—after getting another chip with guac, of course. "So, what are you gonna do?"

"Honestly, I have no idea," Patti says. "It just happened two hours ago. And all I can think is that I won't be able to afford my place anymore. If I can move somewhere cheaper, I can handle the rest until I find another job. Not knowing when that'll be means I need to act fast." She releases a deep breath. "And I just paid my fucking rent too."

"Can you get it back?" I ask her.

She shakes her head. "I don't think so. I have to give thirty days' notice to move anyway, so I have to stay this month."

"What about those new apartments they just built?" Shiree offers. "Those are nice. I've driven by a few times. Even Chaz said he'd live there, and you know what that says."

Patti tilts her head at our friend. "That means either they're super nice and I can't afford to live there or he's hit his fucking head."

Shiree throws a chip at Patti. "Hey! Be nice." But she smiles at her too.

My girlfriend sighs. "I don't think they're move-in ready anyway. The sign outside says their grand opening is in a couple of months."

"Oh!" Lyra exclaims around a mouthful of guac-covered chips. She chews and swallows. "What about my place? It's small, affordable, and almost ready for you to move in. I'll be out in about two weeks."

"You still haven't fully moved out?" I question.

When Blake and Lyra officially started dating after that night he stormed into Shiree's house all caveman-style to claim his woman and his unborn child, he wanted her to move in right away. She partially agreed but kept her place just in case. It's not like she actually stays there for any extended amount of time, so I'm not sure why she hasn't given it up yet. But it's not my business, so I've never asked. Until now.

"Well, I mean, I don't even live there anymore," she answers. Then she eats another chip. "I've just been lazy about boxing everything up and moving it all out. And I refuse to allow someone else to do it. And I refuse to be messy and unorganized about it too. So it's taken me a while. That's all."

Patti wipes under her eyes. "Blake hasn't demanded to help or hire movers?"

"Of course he has," Lyra says, smiling. "It's too bad for him that I'm the one who wears the pants."

Everyone laughs, though it's not as much as before. Then the waiter tries again, and even though we didn't look at menus, we know exactly what they offer and exactly what we want. I order first, and as everyone else tells him what food they want, I get to thinking. By the time they're done, I think I have it all worked out.

"Move in with me," I tell Patti once the waiter is gone.

It's crazy, and she might turn me down, but at least it's out on the table. It's not an unusual offer to make a friend—a best friend—who's down on their luck. And, this way, we won't have to worry about cars in the driveway or making up excuses as to why we drove somewhere together. Plus, I'm ready to take our relationship to the next level, even if no one else even knows we're in it.

She swings her gaze at me. "What?" she asks, one eyebrow raised.

"Move in with me," I repeat, dead serious. "I have the extra room in my house, and it'd get my parents off my back. Surely I'd be 'safe' if I lived with someone else. Then I won't have to get that pet they keep asking about. And we could just split utilities."

"Zo to the rescue!" Shiree exclaims, clapping her hands in front of her, a chip in her hand.

Lyra's nodding a lot, her eyes wide as she grins her approval and chews on some more chips. Even I decide to eat some chips now. For emphasis on my suggestion, I take a single bite of one and smile at her.

"Uh…" While fully facing me, she looks out of the corners of her eyes at our two friends and then flicks her gaze back to me. Then, with that one eyebrow still up, she asks, "Are you sure about that?"

I widen my smile. "One hundred percent sure. It's what best friends do." To punctuate that, I wink.

Her head jerks back in surprise and she blinks at me a few times, but I think it starts to set in. She shakes her head, takes a deep breath, and drops her shoulders. "Okay, then. You'd be saving my life."

"Aww, yay!" Lyra says before taking a sip of her water. "I love our group so much!"

"I do too!" Shiree reaches forward and hugs Lyra. "We're all so awesome."

Patti and I shrug and join in on the hugging. When she embraces me, though, she whispers in my ear so no one else can hear her.

"You swear you're ready for this?"

All I do is nod.

Then she squeezes me tighter. "I love you so much," she says before she sniffles in my ear.

"I love you too, Patti," I tell her.

The girls won't think that's abnormal after everything that just went down, but I honestly don't care. Everyone should know how much I love this woman. And, one day, everyone will. Soon. I swear.

**

Patti

"God, you're so good at that, woman." I release a deep, relaxed exhale as a pulsing orgasm grips my insides and the hot water of the shower beats down on my side. With my back against the wall and my girlfriend's tongue between my legs, I look down and almost come again from the sight alone.

She kisses her way up my torso and boxes me in against the shower all. "Someone lets me get a lot of practice time in." She winks at me.

My gut reaction response is to launch forward and kiss her. When I probe with my tongue, she opens right up and tangles hers with mine. I slide my hands down the sides of her slick, wet body, grip her hips, and slam her against me. Then I bend down and pull one of her nipples into my mouth.

"Hello? Patti?"

I pop my mouth off her and she almost falls backwards out of the shower at the sound of her mother's voice behind my bathroom door. Luckily, my quick reflexes kick in and I grab her by the waist and pull her to me before she tumbles. *What the fuck?* Her parents are supposed to be here later to help me pack. We decided at last week's Friday dinner that we'd have it here at my place on my last night in the apartment. But they're early as fuck. And they apparently let themselves in.

I bring a finger to my lips. "Hey, Ma! I'll be out in just a second."

"Okay!" her mom shouts. "Where's Zo? I saw her car outside, but I don't see her anywhere in here."

"Oh! She's, uh, in the shower!" I tell her.

Zo's eyes are shooting dagger-shaped questions at me. "What the hell?" she mouths.

"Oh, I thought you were in the shower," her mom says.

"No. I already took one. I'm just getting dressed while she showers. She just jumped in."

"Oh. That's…strange. But okay. We brought Chinese. I'll get it set up in the kitchen."

"Thanks, Ma! I'll be out in a minute."

All the color from Zo's face drains, and she looks like she might faint now. In fact, she goes slightly limp in my arms like her knees almost gave out. But I'm still holding her, so I keep her upright as much as I can and grab the bar on the wall to keep us both standing. It takes a few moments, but she finally snaps out of…whatever that was.

"Are you okay?" I whisper loud enough to be heard over the water. "What was that?"

"I'm fine," she says, shaking her head. "You should go though." She backs out of my arms and stands beneath the spray. "Dry off and get out there with them."

"Okay," I say hesitantly. But I pull the curtain back and get out of the shower like she asked me to.

With her parents here, I don't have much of a choice but to keep up appearances. We already almost got caught. We don't need for them to find out before we're ready to tell them, and now just isn't the time. Though it never feels like the time, but now's not the time to think about *that*, either.

As fast as I can, I dry off, dress, and dash out of my bathroom. I head toward the kitchen, and when I round the corner, her mom and her dad are making plates of food for all four of us. They even bought water bottles for us too. The scent of the brown sauce they smother the veggies in helps relax me because I'm starving. But, when they pin me with their gazes, I nearly freeze up again.

I hate keeping secrets from them. And we won't have to forever. For now, though, we are, and the adrenaline from having almost gotten caught is still running through my veins. Which mixes with guilt and fear and makes me feel awful. They aren't my parents. They don't have to be here for me in any capacity. But they have been for as long as I want to remember.

Every time we get together like this, I feel as though I'll be throwing their kindness right in their faces when we tell them we're together. Neither of us wants to break their hearts or destroy them. Yet we both fear that'll happen. At this point, we're both being selfish by keeping to ourselves. It's been easier to deal with by not telling anyone. And it's only going to get easier now that we'll be living together. I have no idea what we're going to do.

"Does Zo shower here often?" her dad asks as he sits at

my kitchen table, a plastic fork in hand.

Mine have since been packed up, so I'm glad they remembered utensils.

"No," I straight-up lie. "We were both just trying to clean up before dinner with you guys. Packing is sweaty business."

"It certainly can be," her mom says before taking a bite of rice and vegetables. "It doesn't seem like you have much left, which is good."

"Very good," I tell her. Then I sit at the table in front of my plate. "We've worked hard this past week, but we tried to keep up with it all month. Between trying to find a job and that, I've stayed busy."

The truth is that all of the important stuff has been at Zo's since the day after that Thirsty Thursday dinner when she offered to move me in. I've spent most of my time there while looking for a job, so packing didn't happen much until this past week. The big stuff I don't need at her house—the couch, the loveseat, this kitchen table—will be in storage until I sell them.

"No luck on the job front?" Her dad looks at me from across the table.

"Not yet. But I've put a lot of résumés out there. It'll happen soon." I smile this time, finally having told the truth for once in this conversation.

"We'll keep praying for you, dear," her mom offers, a genuine smile on her lips.

Which sticks the dagger in a little farther.

Finally, Zo emerges from the bathroom. Her hair is wrapped up in a towel, but she's dressed and looking somewhat normal.

"There you are, Zoeybell." Her dad gets up to hug her.

Rather stiffly, she returns the embrace.

"Everything okay?" he asks quietly.

She nods. "Yep. Just didn't want to be all sweaty when you got here." Then she freezes and looks at me as if to confirm that that's the lie I've already told them.

I press my mouth into a thin line, raise and lower my eyebrows, and give her a small nod. I can see her relief, but I don't think her parents catch it. Her mom's busy eating and her dad was taking his seat again when it happened. All clear. For now.

"You know," her dad continues, "your mom and I were talking on the way here about how you probably won't need to get that dog anymore. Not with Patti in your house."

"No," she agrees while he chuckles at his joke. Then she sits at the table. "Patti will keep me safe, I'm sure." There's barely any emotion behind her words, but I believe she thinks that anyway.

For as long as I possibly can, I'll try my hardest. Though his comment does make me wonder if there's a chance he'll think I'm a suitable person for his daughter to spend her life with. If he thinks she'll be safer at home with me than she'd be alone, that's a good sign, right?

"Until you settle down yourself, Patti. When might that be, you think?" he asks, gathering food on his fork.

Zo starts coughing, and she bangs a fist on her chest to calm her body down. Then she takes a sip from the bottle of water in front of her.

"Well," I start, trying not to laugh, "I think I'll look for a job first. I'm no good to anyone if I'm broke. So I'm really thankful that Zo's taking me in for a while."

Her dad's all smiles. But then the rug is pulled right out from under that idea when her mom speaks up.

"But, honey," she says to her daughter, concern lacing her voice, "aren't you worried people will think you're..." Widening her eyes, she waves a finger between the two of us. "You know."

Zo blinks at her. Several times. I think she knows what her mom is hinting at, but she's not wrong for wanting to gauge her thoughts on this. I, on the other hand, know exactly where she's going with it. Which is why I can barely breathe right now.

"Think we're what, Mom?"

"You know," she repeats, pushing her food around on her plate and staring at her fork like it's really interesting. Then she lowers her voice like the neighbors might hear. "Lesbians."

Zo drops her fork to her plate and rests her forearms on my table. After taking a slow, even breath, she says, "Would that really be so bad?"

"Careful with your tone, Zoeybell," her dad warns. "Don't be rude to your mother, please."

"I'm not being rude," she explains. "I'm just asking. Would it really be that bad if people thought Patti and I were together? It's the twenty-first century, and you love Patti. What's the problem with it?"

"You know exactly what the problem is." Her mom puts her fork down. "Two women don't belong in bed together."

"What about in love, Mom?" she presses while I'm frozen in my chair. "Can two women be together if they're in love?"

Her mom's mouth opens and shuts a couple of times before she clamps her lips together. "I'm not having this pointless discussion with you. You know the difference between right and wrong, and that's all there is to it." She throws her napkin on my table and stands up. "Enjoy the rest of your dinner."

As she leaves the room, her dad looks between the two of us. His gaze is half questioning, half knowing. Under his stare, I want to confess my truth. But I won't do that to Zo, and I hope she won't do that to me right now, either. Yet it seems like we might have nothing to tell now.

He gets up and places his fingertips on my kitchen table. With a resigned expression on his face, he says, "I'm sorry we won't be much help tonight. I should take your mother home." Then he comes around the table and puts his hands on Zo's shoulders, bending to kiss her on her temple. "Love you, Zoeybell." He even does the same to me. "You too, Patti. Goodnight."

The slam of the door behind her parents jolts her, and she squeezes her eyes shut. I want to comfort her, so I reach a hand out to touch hers. She just almost told her parents about us, and while I'm relieved she didn't tell them like that, it's still a secret we have to keep. A secret that we've now confirmed will destroy her family. But, instead of accepting my comfort, she rips her hand away from me.

"Don't," she says quietly. "I just... I can't..." Her hands fly up, palms out, before the tears start.

Again, I attempt to touch her, extending my hand to her shoulder, but again, she pulls away. So I take my hand back and put them both in my lap. Then she gets up and rushes out of the kitchen.

When I find her, she's curled up on my bed. All I have left in this room is my mattress and my dresser. It reminds me that we're about to move in together. To live together as more than roommates. It's yet another way we are solidifying our relationship. Another way we are moving forward and securing ourselves in this. And, after the way her dad reacted, I have more hope than I did before.

So I wrap my arms around her, let her fall apart, and try as hard as I can to transfer the hope I'm feeling to her. She needs it way more than I do right now.

CHAPTER 14

Patti

Zo hums as she wakes up next to me. It's the ninety-second day we've woken up together in the same bed—our bed—but who's counting? Besides those first few days, we've had really great ones. Blissful happiness, truly. I've never felt more sure that she's the one I'm meant to be with, and I thought I was sure when I was sixteen. So that's saying something.

She seems to want this as much as I do too. That's what really makes it special. It's not one-sided anymore. I'm not alone in my feelings. Though I want to shout it to the world, we're still waiting. She's needed more time, and I've never claimed to be an unselfish person, so I've agreed. If not for her, for my own sanity. We decided to make sure we are one hundred percent into this before we create chaos, and we didn't think it'd hurt for her parents to get used to the fact that we live together.

Before Zo opens her eyes, I kiss her sweet lips and pull her against me. I know she's awake, but she has the day off today, so she doesn't want to get out of bed. I don't blame her at all. A day off from work is the perfect excuse to stay comfy all day. But my idea of comfy includes being as close to my woman as possible.

"Good morning," she mumbles against my lips, a small smile curving her mouth.

"Morning," I reply. Then I trail my hand from her back down to her butt and squeeze.

She presses herself closer to me, encircling my neck with her arm. "I love waking up next to you," she says next to my ear.

I roll her on top of me until her knees are on either side of my hips. "I love it too. So much."

Resting her head against my chest, she releases a deep sigh and relaxes. We've done this very thing a few times now, and it's becoming my absolute favorite. Taking a few moments to breathe this moment with her in helps me start my day on a positive, happy note. And I've had more happy days lately than I've ever had. Thanks to her and our life together. I'm pretty sure she'd say the same too, which makes it all that much better.

"I think today's the day," she whispers. Which catches me totally off guard.

Under her, I freeze. Did I hear her right? Is she talking about what I think she's talking about? Can she possibly be ready finally? I mean, I am. I'm ready. Her mom will be upset, but I think her dad can handle her mom and make her see reason. Our friends are a nonissue, but I don't want to falsely reassure her, either. And then—

"Did you hear me?" she says, turning her head and resting her chin on my chest to look up at me.

I crane my head to gaze back at her. "Do you mean it? You're ready?"

She gently nods.

I want to be excited. My body's buzzing with the idea of finally telling everyone we love that we love each other. But I don't want to get my hopes up.

"Why now?" I question.

At first, she simply shrugs. But then she says, "We're more established. We live together. You're employed again.

I think the medication is helping my anxiety." She shrugs again, returning her cheek to my chest. "If we don't do it now, we may never, and I don't want to keep us a secret anymore."

My breath catches in my chest, and my heart thumps beneath her cheek. I'm sure she can feel it, but I don't care. And it's not like I can hide anything from her. I don't want to anyway. She should know how incredible she is to me.

"Hey," I quietly say.

She lifts her head and aims her sleepy gaze at me.

I trace lines up and down her side with my fingers. Then I bring my hand to her face and softly run my knuckles over her cheek. "You're beautiful. I love you." With that same hand, I tuck some of her hair behind her ear. "And, if you're ready, I'm ready."

"I'm ready. I'm terrified, but I'm ready," she says before extending forward and kissing me. Then she pauses with her lips still connected to mine. "Is that my phone buzzing?" She turns her head toward her nightstand.

I don't hear anything, but I'm also riding high on a cloud full of Zo.

She grabs her phone and taps the screen. "Hello?" she asks when she answers it.

I can hear Shiree's frantic voice, but I can't make out what she's saying. I don't have to wait long though. Within thirty seconds, she tells her that we'll be sure to be there, wherever there is, and then hangs up.

"What's going on?" I ask her as she scrambles off the bed.

"Lyra's having her baby, so we're all needed at the hospital." She goes to her dresser and starts dressing her gorgeous, naked body. Which is such a shame.

I prop myself up on my elbows, the sheet pooled at my waist. "Is this a sign? Like today's really supposed to be the day because we're all going to be together?" When I get out of the bed, I head to the closet. It still gives my heart a little jolt when I remember why my clothes are all in here.

"Maybe," she replies, pulling her shirt over her head. Once it's in place, her arms fall to her sides. "Though it's happening a lot sooner than I thought it would and that's freaking me out a little."

I peek out of the closet. "You sounded sure earlier. And it's going to be fine. It's just Shiree and Lyra."

"Right. Lyra." She throws her arms into the air. "Our friend who's in labor. This is the *perfect* time to tell her we're dating." Vigorously, she shakes her head. "Nope. It was a bad idea. The universe is telling us that it's not the right time. We shouldn't do this today."

Well, this isn't how I saw this day going. So I rush over to her, half clothed, and wrap her up in a hug. "Hey. Come back to now, Zed. It's okay. Breathe."

Her body's shaking with her heavy breathing, so I hold her tight to remind her that she's not alone. She doesn't have to do this by herself, and I'll be right there next to her, risking just as much as she is. We're in this together and that's all there is to it.

A minute later, she relaxes. After a deep exhale, she says, "You're right. One step at a time, yeah?"

I peel away to look at her. To make sure she's not just telling me what I want to hear. Honestly, I can't tell. Her anxiety has played tricks on me before, but she's never outright said that she wants to tell everyone. So I nod in response, hug her again, and then finish getting dressed, praying that today's really the day we can come clean and stop living a lie.

***

Zo

present time

"And you know what happened earlier, so..." I shrug

from the same spot on the loveseat. "That's it."

Quietly, so as not to wake her sleeping babies, she claps her hands. "Oh my god!" she mouths to us. She clasps her hands together and smiles. Then she sobers. "I can't believe it's been that long though. I'm sorry you felt like you couldn't tell us."

"You don't have to apologize for anything. That's all me," I tell her.

"Yeah, but you shouldn't have made yourself suffer for it." She gets up when Chaz walks through the door with the food she sent him to get. "I'm glad you finally said something."

Chaz nods and smiles at us as he hands a bag to his wife. "Did I miss the rest of the story?" he asks, walking to the kitchen.

We all follow behind him, and Patti says, "Basically, we're together and scared to tell her parents, but we were ready to tell you guys."

Chaz unpacks the food bags at the kitchen counter. "What's wrong with telling your parents, Zo?"

The whole room goes still, save for Chaz. When he finally realizes it, he does a double take at us.

"Oh wow. It's gonna be that bad?" he asks.

"Charles Masters," Shiree admonishes. "Way to be sensitive."

"Sorry," he starts to say, but then a baby starts to cry. "Oh, shit. I'll go see what's going on."

Shiree takes over, pulling cartons of Chinese food out of a paper bag. My stomach churns though. I didn't want to say anything, but it's food from the same place my parents brought food from that night we got in a fight at Patti's place. We've had Friday dinner since, but my mom has been pretending that the fight never happened. Which has been fine for the most part. I haven't wanted to talk about it. But we're going to have to soon. And the thought makes me sweat with panic.

When the second twin starts crying, Shiree sets a carton on the counter a little harder than she needed to. "I love these kids, you guys. But I'm exhausted."

"We've been here long enough, huh? We can get out of your hair now," Patti tells her, giving her a tight but warm smile. "We'll clean up in here. Go do what you have to do."

"Don't worry about it," she says, coming over to us. She squeezes us both at the same time. "Thanks for trusting us with your secret. We won't say anything until you've told everyone." When she pulls away, she says, "But Lyra's going to be so happy for you two. I promise."

I want to believe her. And I think part of me does. But that doesn't stop my heart from galloping toward a heart attack at the thought of telling more people. We hug her back, though, before she slips away to take care of her twins with her husband.

When we walk outside, Patti takes her phone out of her purse and sends a text. I don't know who it's to, but I don't spend any energy wondering about it. Instead, I get in the passenger's seat and wait for her to sit behind the wheel. Once she does, she looks at me, not yet starting the car.

"Blake said Lyra's up for another visit if you want to finish what we started here. No pressure though. It's totally up to you."

Sure, it's up to me. I can say yes or no. Hope shines in her eyes though. And the last thing I want to do is crush her when she's looking at me like that. So I nod. It's now or never now that we've already told someone.

"Okay. Let's go."

That hope shines even brighter, and even though I'm sweating and shaking a little, I'm starting to feel like I'll do almost anything to keep that hope there in her eyes.

Almost...

CHAPTER 15

Patti

Shiree was right—though post-pregnancy hormones might be to blame too. Lyra squealed, cried, and hugged us so hard. Blake, on the other hand, wasn't surprised in the least. Apparently, he's always thought there was something between us, which is strange considering that the people who know us best were shocked. Happy for us but shocked nonetheless.

We didn't stay long. Visiting hours were almost over when we got there, so we told them and left. Now, we're back in the car, headed for—believe it or not—her parents' house. It was her idea, and she made me drive so she can't chicken out. I think she forgets that I'm just as fucking nervous as she is. But I'm not about to disappoint her right now. She's been so brave today, and I'm super proud of her.

Though I do wonder if she's done too much today by now. Her face is pale, she's deathly silent, and she's staring out the window like she's not seeing anything at all.

"Hey." I put my free hand on her leg. "Talk to me."

She doesn't move. Or speak. So I pat her leg a few times.

"Zed. What can I do?"

"Nothing," she says after a moment. Then she sighs.

"I'm about to lose my parents. But I have you and Shiree and Lyra. That's all I need, right?" Finally, she faces me.

I glance at her before returning my gaze to the road. "Yeah, babe. But I don't think you're going to lose your parents. It's gonna work out, okay?"

It's wishful thinking, but there's no use worrying about it right now. Except we're talking about Zo here. She worries about everything.

"Yeah. Right." She stares out the window again.

I shake her leg. "Come on. So many people are happy for us. That counts for something, right?"

Absentmindedly, she nods. "I don't know if four is 'so many' though," she mutters.

"Kimber's happy too," I say, trying to reassure her. "So there are at least five. Plus us. We're—"

She rounds on me, her head whipping around faster than I thought she could manage right now. "You told Kimber? That barista?"

Oh shit. That was *not* the right thing to say.

"Well, no, not exactly," I start to explain.

"What the heck does that mean?" she spits out at me.

"If you'd let me finish…" Out of the corner of my eye, I peek at her.

She crosses her arms over her chest, waiting for me to do what I asked her to let me do.

"When we were at Thirsty Thursday with Shiree that night and Kimber bought me that drink—"

"She *what?*"

Fucking hell. "Hey. It's no big deal."

"It *is* a big deal, Patti. You didn't tell me that part."

I grip the steering wheel tighter. "Because it's not a big deal! I tried to pay for it myself, but she insisted."

"Why would she even want to buy you a drink?" she asks.

"Probably because I tip her at the coffee shop," I offer.

But she doesn't buy it. "That's what you're *supposed* to

do. That doesn't mean she should buy you a drink."

"She used to do that when we'd see each other out before. That's all," I tell her.

"What?" she shrieks. "Did you, like, date her?"

I want to tell her that she should know this stuff. We were best friends before this, and we talked about everything. But I never gave names because a part of me was always holding out hope that Zo and I would work out someday. And I was trying to avoid this very thing. This jealous-girlfriend routine does not fly with me. Not when Zo knows how much I love her.

"Zo. Calm down. We both have pasts, okay?" I try to reach over to her leg again, but she swats me away. "Oh my god," I breathe out, frustrated. "Yes, we kinda dated or something. But neither of us wanted anything serious. That's all."

"That's not all. You slept with her."

I turn my blinker on to make a right. "You've slept with other people, Zo. Don't make me out to be the bad guy here."

"Yeah, but I didn't sleep with the barista who makes my coffee before I'm even there to pick it up in the morning," she throws in my face.

"For fuck's sake. It's not even like that."

But she won't listen to reason, and she tosses more accusations at me. "Have you slept with her since we got together?"

"Of course not!" I make that right as soon as the light turns green. "And, if that's what you think of me, why are we even going to tell your parents that we're together?"

"We had those weird six weeks, Patti," she reminds me. "Let's not pretend that it's out of the realm of possibility."

"And I spent the whole thing working, waiting for you to come back around, and dreading telling your parents about us."

"Because you'd rather be with Kimber?" she asks, her

voice shaking now.

When I take a second to actually look at her, I see a scared woman. A woman who fears the truth in her words. I don't know what I've done wrong for her not to understand how much she means to me. That she's absolutely it for me. That I've never wanted anyone and won't ever want anyone more than I want her.

With a deep breath, I calm myself down and then approach this in a nicer way. "Of course not, Zed. You are everything I could possibly want and more, okay?" I reach over to put my hand on her leg again, and this time, she lets me. When I squeeze her thigh, I say, "Just you. There's no one else. And there won't ever be. Nothing I've ever done has been easier or more right than being with you. Don't ever doubt us."

She's silent as I park the car in front of her parents' house. Once I'm able, I turn to look at her, and she starts sniffling. As best I can, I gather her into my arms and let her cry. God, this is all so messed up. Love shouldn't be this stressful or hard. Nothing about it should be this difficult. But I have to believe that, in the end, it'll be worth it. When she's not flipping out about ex-flings, she's more than worth it. So I squeeze her tight so she'll feel how much I love her and want to keep her safe. But she's falling apart, trembling in my arms, and I don't want her to face her parents like this.

"I'm sorry," she chokes out between sobs. After sucking a breath in, she says between sniffles, "I don't even know why you like me. I'm a mess."

"Oh, Zed." I tighten my hold on her. "You're the kindness person I know. You want to take care of everyone. You nearly want to save your parents' feelings by resigning yourself to a life without me. You just want everyone to be happy, but you need to see that you deserve to be happy too. And what other people think, including your parents, has nothing to do with you and your happiness. You deserve it just as much as they do."

When I let her go, she's nodding and wiping her eyes.

"I know," she says. "but it's not easy to turn that part of me off. Change isn't easy."

I shake my head. "It's not, but you've been doing it so well. This won't be any different."

She's still pale, and she's clutching her stomach now. "I lied. I'm not ready." She looks at her parents' house before turning back to me. "But it's too late now."

"Do you want me to tell them?" I offer.

It's her turn to shake her head. "No. I need to do this."

"Okay," is all I can say.

When she places her hand on the door handle, she shakes until she grips it and opens the door. I want to pull her back and keep her in the car. Take her back home until she's physically ready to do this. I feel like that's my job—to protect her. She's clearly bad at doing it for herself, and all I want to do is care about her the way she cares for everyone else. I don't think today's the right day anymore, and now, my stomach is doing somersaults as my heart lurches into my throat. Shit.

If I'm this nervous as we walk up to her parents' door, I can't imagine what she's feeling right now.

***

Zo

"Sorry to show up unannounced like this," I tell them as Patti and I enter their house. "We're glad you're home though."

"Okay," my mom says in a strange tone. "What's going on, honey?" She waves to Patti.

"Hey, Ma." Patti gives my mom a hug.

I wait for my mom's attention. Then I ask her, "Can you get Dad?"

"Sure," she replies in that same confused tone. "Have you been crying?"

"Just get Dad, okay?"

She huffs a breath out of her nose, but she does go look for him, so I feel like I have a second to breathe. Until Patti puts a hand on my arm.

"Maybe this isn't a good idea," she whispers when my mom's out of earshot.

My jaw falls open. "Seriously? Are you serious right now?" That came out too loud. My parents probably heard that. "What in the world am I supposed to say to them now?"

"I don't know," she says, "but you don't look okay."

I'm sure she's right. Because I don't *feel* okay, either. I think stress has burned holes in my stomach. Bile's rising up my throat, and my lungs burn like someone lit a match in them. Plus, my head is so light, like it's a balloon rising to the sky. We're here for a reason though. And I've gotten through two other meetings like this. One more can't hurt, right?

At that thought, laughter bubbles up and out of my mouth. That must be the last straw for Patti.

"That's it. Let's go." She takes me by the wrist and starts dragging me toward the door.

My father finds us now though, so I tug her back toward him.

"Zoeybell? What's going on?" he asks, his eyes shining with concern. Then his gaze flicks over my shoulder to Patti and his face loses some color.

I look between the two of them. "What the hell?" I shout.

"Zo! Language!" my mother says, scolding me.

I put a hand up between us and go back to Patti, my chest constricting. "Did you already tell him too?"

"What?" She scrunches her face up. "No, of course not."

"Tell him what, Zo?" my mom asks.

"Beth, maybe you should—"

"No, Jerry. I want to know what my daughter thinks you know," she insists.

My stomach twists as something stabs me from the inside before I can tell her. When I try to take a breath, I can't. Nothing happens.

"Maybe you should sit down," Patti suggests, tugging on my arm.

I attempt to pull out of her grasp, but the movement causes the room to do a full three-sixty around me.

"Zoeybell?" my dad questions. "Come here."

"Jerry, what's wrong with her?" my mom asks.

Then I hear Patti's voice, but I have no idea what she's saying. Something about something not looking right. And that's the last thing that happens before everything becomes too much for my body and the world goes black.

***

Patti

For the third—and the worst—fucking time today, I'm at the hospital. This time, while I wait in the waiting room, the nerves aren't anticipatory. I'm not waiting for my friend to have a baby. I'm waiting to find out what the fuck happened to my girlfriend. And the guilt is eating at me. I just know that it's related to her anxiety. This whole day has been nothing but stress for her, and that's not at all what she needs. I tried to get her to stop, but there was no way to prevent her once she'd started. So here we are.

"The family of Zo Robins?" the doctor who saw her when I took her to the ER the last time asks some two hours later.

I jump up, but so do her parents. The same parents who said exactly nothing to me the entire time we were waiting.

The same parents who speak to the doctor as if I'm not here.

"That's us," her dad says.

"Great." The doctor looks at his chart. "Zo is stable. She's not awake yet, but she's resting comfortably."

"Thank God." Her mom's watery eyes close, and she brings a hand to her mouth. "Will she wake up soon?"

"We think so," the doctor says. "If you want to sit with her, I'll take you back there."

"That'd be great. Thank you." Her dad takes her mom's hand and starts to follow the doctor.

I do too, but when her mom turns around, she stops walking.

"Not you. I'm sure it's family only," she says to me.

My heart stops. I *am* family. I'm the closest thing to family and unconditional love Zo has. And she wants to stop me from seeing my own girlfriend? She has to be fucking kidding.

"Oh, I thought you were family," the doctor says, pointing the manila folder at me. "Weren't you…" But he trails off, leaving out the part that says he clearly remembers me from when I brought Zo here before.

"She's just a friend of the family," her mom says, a hard edge to her tone. "She can stay out here."

I open my mouth to let her have it because this is ridiculous, but nothing comes out. I don't say a word. Instead, my mouth closes and I look at Zo's dad as a last-second plea for help. The understanding but helpless expression on his face slices through me. There's nothing he can do, and the doctor can't do anything, either. So they all walk away and leave me standing here alone, like I haven't been a part of this family for the last fourteen years. Like I don't love their daughter more than life itself. Like their daughter doesn't love me too.

Reluctantly, I go back to the seat I was occupying before the doctor came out. And I stay here, not wanting to get up even for coffee, in case the doctor comes back and lets me go see her. And an hour and a half later, the doctor *does* come back. As soon as I see him, I'm up and out of my seat.

"Patti, right?" he asks, his hand in his coat pocket.

I nod. "Is she okay?"

"She will be. But she's asking for you," he says.

Immediately, I start walking back toward where I think her room is. When I realize I need him to show me, I stop. He chuckles a little before passing me and waving for me to follow him.

"How do you two know each other?" he asks while we walk.

"She's my girlfriend," I tell him like it's the natural answer I've been using for years. I don't care who knows anymore.

Her parents had a chance, and they don't even deserve the truth. At least, her mom doesn't. She's under my skin right now, and it's going to take everything I have not to walk in there with guns blazing. For Zo, I'll stay calm though.

"That's what I thought the first time I saw her." He leads me around a corner. "Her parents don't like it?"

"They don't exactly know yet," I admit. "We were trying to tell them when she passed out."

When we reach her door, he says, "Oh wow. Yeah, she definitely needs to keep her stress down. She also needs to heal a small ulcer in her stomach. What she needs is rest. So take care of her, okay?" He smiles at me before knocking on the door and letting us in.

A fucking ulcer? For fuck's sake. This woman is literally falling apart by keeping our secret.

Which is the last thing I get to contemplate before I walk into the room and Zo starts hysterically crying. So I bolt to her bed and take her hand in mine. Her parents are on the other side of her bed, staring at the two of us as I comfort their daughter.

"I'm so sorry they wouldn't let you back here," Zo sobs into my shoulder.

"Shh," I coo. "Everything's okay, babe. I'm here now."

"Zo," the doctor says, "can we get you anything right now? How are you feeling?"

She sniffles against me but tells him, "I'm better now. Thank you for getting her."

He smiles kindly. "No problem. We need you at a lower level of stress though, okay? So take some deep breaths for me. Then I'll stop bothering you," he tells her, finishing with a wink in our direction.

She listens, breathing in deep through her nose, holding it for a few seconds, and then letting it go out of her mouth. After a third time, she stops shaking and crying, and I'm suddenly holding a much less upset woman in my arms. Thank fuck.

I give her a squeeze. "Great job."

She hugs me back the best she can in this awkward position.

The doctor grins at her. "That's wonderful. Keep doing that when you get too worked up, okay? We'll check up on you later, then. And don't forget to push the call button if you need anything." He nods once and then makes his exit.

Man, I like that guy. Someone needs to have Zo's best interests in mind. Someone besides me. So I'm glad she has him in her corner.

My attention is snapped back to the situation at hand when Zo grabs my hand, the one I don't have around her shoulder, and clears her throat.

"Mom. Dad," she says.

My stomach clenches. Maybe I have an ulcer too from all of this shit.

"What is it, honey?" her mom asks. "What's so important after you just woke up from passing out that you needed Patti and you need to tell us right now?"

"Zoeybell, you should probably get your rest first," her

dad tries, but Zo won't hear it.

"No," she says, squeezing my fingers until I think they might break. "I need to tell you. We need to tell you. Right now. I'm sick—literally—of keeping this a secret." Her heart rate monitor beeps more rapidly, but she ignores it and pushes on. "Patti and I love each other." Once the words are out, she releases a huge breath and sags against me.

Holy hell. She said it. It's out there. And I hold her tight, proud of her for having said it. Her father's eyes slowly close like he knew this was coming but isn't looking forward to watching the wreckage. Yet her mom doesn't understand the depth of the words.

"Of course you do, honey. She's been your sister since—"

"No, Mom. She's not my fucking sister."

Whoa. Maybe I'm not a great influence on her. I don't think I've ever heard her say that word.

"Zo! Language!" her mom reprimands.

"No, Mom," Zo says again. "I'm a grown woman. And I love another woman. And I could have died from keeping this a secret. I won't do it anymore, and if you don't understand, then you can leave."

Her mom's forehead scrunches up as she stares at her daughter like she's grown three heads. "Maybe you're confused because you've spent so much time together now that you're roommates."

"We're not fucking roommates, either," Zo spits out at her. "We're together. A couple. And we're going to get married."

I whip my head in her direction, my eyes wide as hell. "We're what?"

At the same time, her mother also shouts, "You're what?"

And, out of the corner of my eye, I see her father's eyes fly open.

"I'm sorry. I should have said something before, but I kind of passed out," Zo says to me. "I want to marry you. I want us to get married. And I'm sorry I'm rambling, but this all needs to come out. I've been holding way too much in, and now, I'm here. In the hospital." Her head falls back onto the bed.

"Zo," her mom says, all seriousness. "You can't marry Patti."

"And why not?" she throws back at her mother. "Because she's a woman?"

"Exactly." Her mom crosses her arms over her chest. "That's exactly why. Tell her, Jerry."

Her dad stays silent though.

"Jerry. Tell our daughter she's not marrying another woman."

When he still doesn't say anything, I decide to speak up.

"Um, I'm not just some woman. Let's not forget that." I sit up straighter on the bed, my arm staying around Zo for strength—we both need it. "I've been here for her since we were freshmen in high school. I've loved her since I was sixteen. I've always known we'd end up together even if you haven't. Even if Zo hasn't. But she realizes it now, and I'm not a stranger in your life. I'm practically your daughter too."

"All the more reason why this is so wrong!" her mom shouts. "You're practically family!"

"That's funny," I say, barely keeping my cool. "I wasn't anything close to family when it came time to see Zo. Now that she wants to be my wife, I'm too much like family? You can't have it both ways, Ma."

"I won't listen to this. It's wrong and disgusting and I won't stand for it."

"It doesn't matter if you won't stand for it, Mom," Zo quietly says. There's a soft strength in her voice. "I love Patti, she loves me, and we're getting married." Then she looks up at me as if to confirm that last point.

With tears in my eyes, I smile and nod, squeezing her close to me.

She aims her strong gaze back at her mom. "I don't know when yet, but I'd like for you to be at our wedding."

Her mom scoffs. "This is ridiculous. Let's go, Jerry." Without looking back, she storms out of the room.

Her father, though, gives us a sympathetic frown. He swallows hard, his Adam's apple bobbing from the effort. "I love you both so much, and I wish this were different." Then he pats Zo's leg, tucks his hands in his pockets, and follows his wife through the door.

I expect Zo to fall apart. I wait on pins and needles for her to start sobbing yet again in my arms. But, to my surprise, she doesn't. She takes a deep, soothing breath through her nose, holds it, and slowly releases it through her mouth.

"We're really getting married?" she asks. "That actually happened, right?"

This time, I'm the one who's crying. "Oh my god, Zed. That *did* happen. You really mean it?"

She nods, resting her head against mine. "I should have said something before. Honestly, I don't know how this stuff works."

"Whatever feels good and right to you. Always. Just say the word."

After a moment, she says, "Marriage. That feels good and right."

My body shudders with a sob. The love of my life wants to marry me. And she told her parents. And the worst happened, but we're still here. She may be in the hospital, but I'm going to make sure she gets better. Together, we're going to figure this stuff with her parents out. I think her dad's on our side, and he'll help her mom see the light. But, in the meantime, we have each other.

And, apparently, we have a wedding to plan.

EPILOGUE

Patti

Six months later

"Come back to now, Zed." I rub her back in a soothing rhythm, though I'm not sure it's working.

She's laughing too hard to relax, and it's becoming contagious. Soon, I double over, unable to control myself. Shiree's howling and snorting, but Lyra's giggling is silent, and we're all so lost to the humor of the moment.

"That really happened?" Shiree asked between laughing fits.

Lyra nods, still giggling. After a breath, she says, "It did! You should have seen Blake's face. There was…" She loses it again, bending forward at the waist. But she's able to squeak the rest out in a high-pitched voice. "Poop was everywhere!" Big breath. "On Xavier."

Oh yeah. They finally named their son after three long days. It took a game of Rock, Paper, Scissors, best of five, to settle it. Though I have a sneaking suspicion Blake would have given Lyra her way in the end anyway.

Another gasping breath. "On the walls," Lyra chokes out. More laugher. More breathing. "On *Blake!*"

Each of us laughs even harder than before, and though part of me worries about Zo and her anxiety, I love seeing her looking so happy and carefree. So far, so good, so I allow myself to enjoy this moment with her and our two friends.

"Oh my god!" Shiree exclaims. "I can't..." She gasps for breath.

Zo squeezes my hand, smiling so wide and waving the other one in the air. When she finally can, she rushes her words out. "What's he gonna do with another baby?"

Lyra places her hand on her belly as she calms a little. "Oh, girl. I have no idea, but we're going to find out soon."

"It's a good thing you two already got married," Shiree says. "You wouldn't want to fit a wedding dress around your growing belly."

And there's my segue. "Speaking of getting married... Think we can get this show on the road now?" I poke my soon-to-be wife in her side, smiling at her.

Reluctantly, she stands up from the couch in our living room. She glances at the front door before sticking her hand out to me. "Absolutely."

I take her hand and rise. She's waiting for her parents. I know this. Lyra and Shiree know this. But we've waited long enough. It's an hour past the time we told them we would start and they're not here. So we all look at each other with sympathetic but supportive expressions and decide to get a move on.

Lyra takes Zo back to our bedroom to get dressed. I head to the spare room with Shiree. Zo decided on a more traditional wedding dress, whereas I went with something shorter and spunkier but no less white—though it has a splash of light blue, just like hers will have purple. We haven't shown each other the dresses. It's bad luck to see a bride's wedding dress before the wedding. Which means both brides kept them secret. Very soon, though, I'll get to see how stunning she is. Just like she is to me every day.

Once Shiree has zipped me up, we walk to the backyard, where Chaz, Blake, and all the babies are waiting. Our officiant is all set up too, and most of the chairs are full. When everyone's out here, two might still be vacant, but I can't say I'm not holding out hope.

The past six months have been both wonderful and rather difficult. Seeing as Zo and I are getting married today, our relationship has been spectacular. I've been gainfully employed, and her health has steadily improved as well. She's off all medication already, and she hasn't had a panic attack in seventeen weeks. The last one was when we finally had the conversation she wanted to wait until "later" to have that day at Shiree's when we told them about us.

We were at our first Thirsty Thursday since our friends had had their babies, all out as a big group. Spouses, babies—all of us. We've done it like that ever since, but this one naturally brought up the baby conversation. When it was directed toward Zo and me, she froze. So I answered for us. But my, "I don't think so," response wasn't at all okay with her. Apparently, she's always wanted kids, more than she's ever let on. But, being that I can't give her one, she wasn't sure how that was going to work out. And she hadn't brought it up because she didn't know. Plus, she worried it'd freak me out so early into our relationship. Instead, it all came to a head at dinner with our friends.

I've always known I wanted to be with her. And I understand how reproduction works. So I guess I assumed we probably wouldn't have kids. I wasn't opposed to that cat or dog she wanted, but I'd taken kids off the table a long time ago. Until I saw and heard how much she wanted them. She ended up running out of the restaurant, frustrated with how I'd reacted. When I finally got her to calm down—with reminders of how well her ulcer was healing and that she shouldn't get worked up over something we could calmly discuss—we talked it through. I explained my side and happily agreed to somehow have a baby with her, no matter what it took, if it was that important to her. All I want is her happiness, and any child would be so lucky to have her as their mother. And I think I have just the thing to prove how I feel about it to her too. But I'm saving that for later.

The most difficult part of the last six months has been not having any relationship with her parents. Unfortunately, everything went exactly how she'd feared it would. They haven't spoken to us since everything happened in the hospital that day. But we both know her parents well enough to think they wouldn't possibly miss this day. Her mom would regret it more than she'd gain by not being here. I guess we'll see soon.

When it's time, I stand up near the officiant and wait for my bride. We decided to do it this way so the wedding would seem more traditional to her parents. They may not be here, but it sounded important to Zo anyway. Shiree snaps some photos before she heads back to the house to get Zo. She and Lyra will walk her down the aisle, and I can't wait.

But, when Shiree and Lyra come back outside without Zo, I start to panic. Did she change her mind? Is she having a panic attack? Do I need to call 911? Just as I start to bolt toward the house, Lyra stops me.

"Everything's fine," she says, a hand in the air. "Stay there." Then she smiles at me, which does its job and relaxes my worries.

But what made the plan change? Why aren't they bringing my bride out? Where is she, and what's going on?

The answers come when the back door opens and she steps out through it, her dad on one arm and her mom on the other.

***

Zo

Five minutes earlier

Lyra ties my dress up in the back. I'm not sure I can breathe anymore, but it's not from how tight the bodice is. It's way more about the fact that my parents are actually going to miss my wedding. But it's also about the fact that it doesn't matter. I'm going through with it whether they're here or not. Patti and I belong together even if they don't approve. Our friends are here to support us, and I couldn't ask for more than that. Well, I could, but I won't.

"All done! My goodness, Zo. You're absolutely gorgeous," Lyra says over my shoulder, into the mirror. She sets a hand on my bare shoulder, tears shining in her eyes. "Sorry. This pregnancy already has me overemotional." She wipes under one eye. "I'll go freshen up before we walk you down the aisle." With a smile, she darts out of my room and heads to the bathroom.

When the door shuts behind her, I gaze into the mirror and smooth my hands down the front of my dress. If I think too hard, I'll need to freshen up the makeup Patti worked so hard to do for me. And we can't have that. I wouldn't know the first thing on how to do that. So I shut my eyes, take a deep, cleansing breath, hold it in, and then release it through my nose.

Someone knocks on the door, and when I look into the mirror as it opens, I expect to see Lyra, maybe even Shiree. Neither of them appears in the reflection before me though. Instead, my father is staring back at me. He's dressed in a black suit, his tie perfectly knotted around his neck. And, if I thought it was hard to breathe before, I'm completely out of air now.

"Dad?" I say when I've spun around to face him.

"Hey, Zoeybell. Looks like we haven't missed anything?"

I run into his arms and squeeze him around his middle. "I'm so glad you're here," I whisper against his chest. Then I shoot my gaze up to his. "Wait. Is…"

When I trail off, he kisses my forehead. Then he

releases me and holds his arm out in a gesture for me to go see for myself. Once I'm out of my room, I dash down the hall—the best I can in this dress, anyway—and then skid to a stop when I reach my living room. There, in her Sunday best on a Saturday afternoon, stoically stands my mother.

Slowly, I walk up to her, holding my dress up so it doesn't get ruined. My mother's face softens as I approach her, and she goes from crossed arms to tears in her eyes before I'm right in front of her.

"Oh, Zo," she sighs. "I can't say I approve, but a mother can't miss her daughter's wedding."

I've waited for this moment. Probably for all of my life. Every little girl dreams of her wedding. I don't think any little girl dreams of it happening like this, but this is the hand I've been dealt. This is the culmination of all of my choices. And I thought I'd be more upset that she still doesn't approve of my life. I'm not though. She's here, and that's good enough for now.

So I hug her. Tight. "Thank you for being here."

Hesitantly, she returns my embrace, but she says nothing else. Which is okay. I kiss her cheek and then let her go, holding my elbow out for her. She takes a few moments to decide, but ultimately, she loops her arm through mine, even going so far as to squeeze mine to her. Then I turn toward my father and offer him my other arm, which he takes, tears in his eyes.

"You look beautiful, Zoeybell." He smiles down at me.

"Thank you." I grin back at him and then look at my mom. "I'm so glad you're both here."

I swear that the smallest hint of an upward curve lifts her lips. That gives me hope even if I shouldn't let it take flight. So I run with it, ushering us out the back door and down the aisle, toward my bride, my friends, and the rest of my life.

~~~

After the ceremony is over and the photos have been

taken, Patti, Shiree, Lyra, Chaz, Blake, and I eat a good meal in the backyard, around a large table we rented for the occasion. My parents left after pictures, which didn't make me as sad as I'd thought it would. Though it was nice to have them here for our big day, I'm glad the crowd has thinned to people who truly love and support us in everything we do.

"So," Blake says, putting an arm around his wife's shoulder. "Who's changing their last name?"

Lyra swats at him. "Oh my god! You can't just ask them that!"

He shrugs and sticks his bottom lip out. "Why not?" Then he points to us. "Do you guys care? Did that offend you?"

Laughing, we both shake our heads. But Patti's the one who fields the question.

"Actually," she replies once she's done giggling at our friends' antics, "we've decided to leave the names. Zed here doesn't want to hammer the final nail in her mother's coffin, so we're leaving that alone for the time being."

"And then what?" Chaz questions.

Shiree swats at her husband now. "Charles Masters. That's none of our business."

"Oh please." He gets up to hold one of the twins when they start to cry. "Don't pretend like you didn't want to know."

Shiree and Lyra turn shades of red as they sputter out nonsense about how it's not polite to ask and waiting until information is voluntarily made available.

"Yeah, right." Blake sits back in his chair, grinning. "That's not how you women work. You're not fooling anyone."

"How's life as the CEO?" I ask loudly to deflect that conversation. Though I worry a lot less these days, I still have my moments.

"Great," he says. "Every now and then, I get this guy's

advice." He points to Chaz. "But things are looking good."

"It's funny," Chaz responds, his son in his arms. "They wanted a family man, ended up with you, and still got a family man. It's crazy how things work." He winks at Blake.

Who balls his napkin up and throws it at Chaz. "Speak for yourself. Look at you, Mr. Husband and Father Of Twins."

Chaz's smile is proud as he kisses his wife's cheek and sits back down. "Damn straight."

"Do you have to swear around the babies?" Shiree asks, but she hardly looks that upset about it.

"Apparently, it's the night of pretending you're a saint." Then he winks at his wife, which earns a significantly different reaction than his wink to Blake did.

Patti rests against the back of her chair and takes my hand. She brings it to her lips and kisses it. "Hey," she quietly says to me while the rest of the table bickers and rocks babies. "I have a wedding gift for you."

I gasp, my free hand flying to my mouth. "You do? You didn't have to do that! I didn't—"

She laughs lightly. "Stop. Really, it's for both of us, so no freaking out. Okay?"

Dropping my hand to my lap, I nod. Once she's gestured her head back toward the house, she gets up, and I trail behind her. The table goes quiet, but then their voices grow loud again with conversation that sounds forced and made up. Clearly, they're allowing the newlyweds some privacy. But that's not what this is, right? She isn't seriously giving me sex for a wedding present. Though that could be considered something for both of us...

No. That's definitely not it. When I round the corner to enter the guest room, my heart can't decide if it wants to sprint to a finish line or stop altogether. Ultimately, it keeps going. This woman gives it life again and again, and it looks like this house might have new life in it soon.

With a hand to my mouth, I slowly say, "This is why

you kept me out of here all week? It wasn't because of your dress?"

She shakes her head. Then she wraps her arms around me from behind. "Nope. I want you to have everything you want. And this is something I can give you. Somehow, someway, you'll be a mother. We both will."

"Really?" I ask before spinning around in her arms.

She wipes under my right eye. "Absolutely. I saw how you were with the twins. And you've been great with Xavier too. As much as I want to be selfish and keep your love all to myself, it's clear to see you are meant to do so much more." Her soft lips land on my mouth. "So we better get busy and practice making a baby."

I burst into laughter. "Um, babe, I don't think that's how it works."

"Eh." She shrugs. "It's worth a shot, right?"

My grin is so wide that my cheeks hurt. But I wouldn't have it any other way. "Everything with you," I promise her, touching my nose to hers, "is worth a shot."

SNEAK PEEK OF
THE BARISTA'S WAGER BABY
Book 4 in the Thirsty Thursday series

CHAPTER 1

Kimber

Monday mornings are my favorite. I know, I know. That sounds crazy. But hear me out. Working at a coffee shop makes Monday mornings awesome. It's the busiest morning of the week, so I see nearly all of my regulars. And my regulars are totally awesome people. For the most part. We get a few who definitely aren't morning people by any stretch of the phrase, but in general, everyone's cool. I mean, who isn't cool to the person pouring your morning cup of caffeine, right?

Even though they're busy and rushed, Monday mornings tend to start a little later, which makes me happy. And today starts off no differently than every other Monday. Once I've opened the shop, started the coffee, set the ready pastries out in the case, and popped new pastries into the oven with the help of our chef, Eileen, I wait for the chaos with a smile on my face.

Here is when this Monday deviates from all others in the past though. Patti Caraway, a former fling and a woman I haven't seen in over a year, walks into The Steam Room technically before we're even open. Bright and early on a Monday morning. Which is something I've never seen and never thought I'd see.

"Hey, lady! I didn't expect to see you today," I tell her. "Want the usual?"

"Please!" she says enthusiastically, clasping her hands in front of her.

I get to work pouring her a cup—black with a dash of cocoa. While I'm stirring, she stops approaching when she's three feet away from the counter.

"Wait. You remember how I like my coffee?" She puts a hand on her hip. "After all this time?"

With my index finger, I tap my temple. Then I cap her to-go cup. "Once it's up here, it never leaves." That's punctuated with a wink.

"Kimber! You're a peach!" she exclaims—just like she used to when she came in regularly.

"What can I say?" I shrug and set her coffee on the counter. "It's a gift."

She hands her debit card over. "Have you ever considered opening up your own shop? You'd be really fucking good at it."

I punch the total in and ring the sale up. While I'm grabbing a lemon poppy seed muffin, I say, "Nah. I wouldn't want to compete with this place. And it's a lot of work to start from the ground up." Once the muffin is in a paper bag so she can take it with her, I hand it over. "For Zo." And I give her another wink.

"Seriously?" she asks, taking the bag. "You are way too nice this early in the morning."

"It's no problem." Smiling genuinely, I ask, "How is she? I think I heard something about adoption, right?"

"Yes!" She slaps a hand on the counter and palms her coffee cup to raise it in the air. "Which is why I need this. Today's the day we finally get to meet our daughter!"

"Oh, how exciting!" I go around the counter to give my

friend a hug. "I'm so happy for you!" When I pull away, I shake my head a little. "Though I have to say that I never saw you married with kids. But hey. Life surprises us, right?"

Patti laughs. "I know! Already a year married. And we're having a baby today." Then she brings her coffee cup to her lips and takes a shaky sip. "Holy shit. We're having a baby today."

I rest a hand on her shoulder. "And you're going to be great mothers."

"Zo definitely will," she replies, staring at the wall. "But this might be my last hot cup of coffee." She takes another sip.

Maybe this would scare other people, but this is yet another reason why I love working in this coffee shop. My customers trust me. They tell me nearly everything, and I'm able to help them through hard times and celebrate good ones. Being there for people brings me joy. And, even though Patti and I have a romantic history, that's all in the past. I still care about her as a person and want the best for her. Which is her wife, who's the absolute love of her life, and her upcoming daughter.

"I think I might know a place that can help in that department." I toss a smile over my shoulder as I head back around the counter.

She takes a deep breath, holds it, and then slowly releases it through her mouth. Then her face relaxes. "Wow. That really does work. I was onto something every time I told Zo to do that."

"See?" I say. "It's going to be fine."

After a rushed-out exhale, she swallows more coffee. "Enough about me. What about you? Seeing anyone?"

I wave a dismissive hand before crossing my arms over my chest. "Eh. Nothing worth mentioning." Then I shrug one shoulder.

"Aww, really?" She frowns. "I never would have thought I'd be the one settled down out of the two of us."

A light laugh escapes my lips. Though it's mostly for show. "I know, right?" Then a smile curves my lips, but it's a little sad. "I've dated a little. A guy here, a girl there. But nothing's really stuck. And I'm so busy with this place." I gesture a hand around the building.

Both of us look toward the front of the coffee shop when the door opens and the bell on top jingles. When I don't recognize the man in the suit entering through the door, I glance at my watch to make sure we're actually open this time. It isn't like I'd turn a customer away, but it's a good thing to remember.

However, when Patti turns back to face me, her eyes are wide and her smile's just as big. "Maybe you'll make some time soon," she says mischievously. She winks and then holds the bag and her coffee up in the air. "Thanks. We'll catch up soon, okay?" After one last huge grin, she spins around, nods at the man approaching the counter, and heads out the door.

Inwardly, I roll my eyes at her, but I'm smiling too. She's probably still "honeymoon" happy, but that doesn't mean I can't be hopeful of good things to come. Even if it's not of the romantic kind. It's a good Monday, but I wasn't kidding when I said I'm busy with this place. And the morning rush starts now.

***

Jordan

For fuck's sake. Why is my phone ringing so goddamn early? When I grab it off my bedside table, my dad's name is lighting the screen up. I don't know why he thinks he needs to call me right now, but I guarantee he doesn't.

"Hello?" I say when I answer, sleep making my voice gravelly.

"Did I wake you up?"

"Of course you woke me up." I throw an arm over my forehead. "It's five in the morning."

"It's *six*. You're about to be late on your first day."

I roll over and check the clock. Well, he's right. I'll give him that. But I still don't need to be up right now. I could and should still be sleeping.

"I'm not going to be late, Dad. I'm twenty-five years old. You don't have to treat me like I'm fifteen."

"Son, this isn't New York City. There's no on-time train to catch to get you there at the last second. You have to get yourself there on time."

After I sigh, I tell him, "And I will."

"You won't at this rate because you have to stop on the way to pick up breakfast and coffee to make the right impression on your coworkers."

I roll my eyes. "Seriously? It's not enough that I'll be wearing a tie with my suit?"

It's his turn to sigh. "This is exactly why I had to pull strings for you to get a job."

"Whoa," immediately comes out of my mouth. "I didn't ask you to pull strings, and I was fully capable of getting a job. It just wasn't up to your standards."

"My standards will make you successful, son. That's what you need right now. Something good to focus on now that you're back home and ready to make something of yourself." After a short beat of silence, he adds, "And I'm sure you didn't remember to get a haircut…"

This conversation is going nowhere. It's the same one we've had since I moved home. Never mind that I had enough money saved up from my last job to get here, rent a place, and spend a month looking for work. None of that matters as much to him as a son with a "successful" job. And this conversation will never end if I don't make it stop. So I take a deep breath, blow it out, and concede. Like I always do. It's easier than fighting.

"You're right, Dad. Where should I stop to get coffee?"

~ ~ ~

Maybe, if I'd gotten laid just *once* in the last month, I wouldn't be so grumpy right now. But I'm fucking grumpy. I'm headed to a coffee shop so I can pick up coffee and pastries for people I don't even know. People who work for a company I don't give two shits about. And I have to do a job I don't give even one shit about.

Okay, that's just me being grumpy about my dad and his meddling. They're probably perfectly nice people who work at a perfectly nice place I don't want to work at. That's all. Hopefully this coffee shop has good coffee. And won't screw my order up. I could fucking use it right now.

I pull my car—the one I was able to buy by myself when I moved back home—up in front of The Steam Room. When I get out, I adjust my stupid tie. I can't believe I have a job where I have to wear a tie. In fact, why were ties even invented? And why are they still a thing now?

Good god. I need to calm down. This is only day one of the rest of my dull, boring existence. I better get used to it now while I can.

When I open the door, the smell of something sweet baking in the oven hits me first. Then the rich scent of brewing coffee overrides it. Maybe today won't be so bad after all. Coffee is always the answer. And a good pastry never hurts.

"Thanks. We'll catch up soon, okay?" a woman with short, black hair says. Then she walks past me on her way to the door, giving me a weird nod, which I catch when I glance up at her.

That throws me off as I reach into my back pocket for wallet. I fumble for it, and when I've finally retrieved it, it slips out of my hands and lands with a thunk on the tile. Goddammit. It's way too early for this shit. Could this day get any worse?

162

ABOUT THE AUTHOR

kyle autumn

Kyle Autumn is the author of sexy contemporary romances that will melt your heart and your panties. She also writes erotic short stories series that will likely melt your panties more than your heart. She loves chocolate and pajamas. Can't be bothered to brush her hair most days. Can always be bothered to write her pants—er, pajama bottoms—off.

Manufactured by Amazon.ca
Bolton, ON

12977028R00099